DEATH WARRIORS

When geologist and big game hunter
Rex Brandon sets off into the African
jungle to prospect for a rare mineral,
he is prepared for danger — two previous expeditions on the same mission
mysteriously disappeared, never to return.
But Brandon little realises what hor-
rors his own safari will be exposed
to . . . He must deal with the treachery
and desertion of his own men, hunt a
gorilla gone rogue, and most terrify-
ingly of all, face an attack by ghostly
warriors in the Valley of Devils . . .

DENIS HUGHES

◆

DEATH
WARRIORS

Complete and Unabridged

LINFORD
Leicester

First published in Great Britain

First Linford Edition
published 2017

A catalogue record for this book is available
from the British Library.

ISBN 978–1–4448–3204–4

Published by
F. A. Thorpe (Publishing)
Anstey, Leicestershire

Set by Words & Graphics Ltd.
Anstey, Leicestershire
Printed and bound in Great Britain by
T. J. International Ltd., Padstow, Cornwall

This book is printed on acid-free paper

1

Seekers Die

Winging north from the coast, the air-craft flew over dense mangrove swamp and tangled jungle country. Here and there it passed over small clearings, each with its cluster of round thatched dwell-ings and groups of natives who stared upwards, open-mouthed, at the silver-winged machine as it roared overhead.

Despite the fact that they were travelling swiftly, the two men in the cabin of the plane were conscious of the steamy heat that rose in waves from the ground beneath them. It caught the aircraft and lifted it, only to drop it again with a sickening bump a few seconds later.

The pilot, a lanky young man with sun-bleached hair and a ready smile, glanced sideways at his passenger.

'Just about ten more minutes, Mr. Brandon,' he said. 'Mandibarza will be hot as an oven!'

Rex Brandon stared ahead through the curved Perspex shield in front of him. The thought that a few more minutes would see the first stage of his journey completed brought a sense of excitement to him. Experienced as he was, there was always a recurrence of that first excitement whenever he started a new adventure. Brandon was the sort of man who made adventure from even the ordinary, everyday things of life. There was some quality about him which prompted friends to say he was born a century too late. By rights he should have been in the ranks of the early pioneers, exploring, probing, seeking to wrest the secrets from the dark silent places of the earth. But even so, Brandon, in the prime of life, made adventure for himself.

Now he leaned forward slightly in his seat, straining his shoulders against the safety straps as he peered ahead through the steamy haze that rose from tracts of jungle below. The distorted shadow of the aircraft bobbed and jerked as it sped across the dark green tree-tops to starboard.

The young pilot shot another glance at

his passenger. This was the first occasion on which he had met Rex Brandon, but the fame of the well-known geologist and big game hunter was legendary. The pilot was aware of the extraordinary strength of Brandon's character. He admired him a great deal, and would have given a lot to have been able to join him for the duration of whatever mysterious trip Brandon meant to undertake in the almost unexplored interior that lay ahead. But Trevor was only a charter pilot. He sighed and gave his whole attention to the task of taking his aircraft across the jungles of Nigeria towards Mandibarza.

Brandon, for his part, quietly acknowledged the skill with which Trevor did his job. But his mind was busy with other things. Why, for instance, had he been summoned so mysteriously to Mandibarza by a man of international importance? It was a question he could barely wait to have answered. The answer would be forthcoming when the plane eventually landed on the narrow airstrip. But Brandon was still impatient. He disliked impatience on principle, yet there were times when he fell a victim to it himself. A wry smile crossed his sun-burnt features for a moment. No man was perfect, he reflected. He relaxed in his seat again.

'Queer what a fascination the most uncomfortable places of the world have for men,' he remarked. 'These jungles, for example ... No one could call them attractive, yet a lot of men spend a considerable amount of time in cutting a way through them. Why, I wonder?'

Trevor grinned boyishly. It was the first time Brandon had spoken more than a few words since taking off from Lagos.

'I was thinking the same thing myself a few days ago,' he replied. 'I still don't know the answer.' He glanced at the compass above his head, checking automatically.

'Something to do with a sense of attainment I suppose,' said Brandon. 'What's Mandibarza like? I've never been there before.'

Trevor grinned again. 'Half a dozen bungalows, a lot of native huts and the airstrip. That's about all — apart from mosquitos, flies and heat, of course!'

Brandon nodded. 'More or less what I

expected,' he said.

'Excuse me asking,' went on Trevor, 'but is this a big game expedition you're going on?'

Brandon hid a smile. He doubted if game was to be his only object in the interior, but guarded instructions had told him that big game would do as a cover for whatever else he was to undertake.

'Yes,' he said softly. 'Plenty of game in these forests. I might even bag a gorilla or two.'

Two or three minutes later a break appeared in the dark green mantle of foliage ahead. Trevor gave a satisfied grunt. They were dead on course.

'There's your destination, Mr. Brandon,' he said

The plane began to drop at a steep angle as Trevor went in to approach. Cut from the steamy haze of forest that hemmed in the little settlement of Mandibarza, the airstrip was exactly like a length of dirty ribbon stretched out on the ground. At one end of it, nearest the town, stood a wooden bungalow, starkly white against the shadowed ground. A long veranda fronted the building, its corrugated iron roof offering some slight relief from the intense heat.

As Trevor brought the plane down low at the far end of the runway, Brandon caught sight of a big Ford station wagon rolling to a halt by the bungalow.

'That's the charter company's office,' said Trevor. 'Fellow named Barnet runs it. He was more or less the man who started the service out here. Nice chap. No one thought an airline route to Mandibarza would be worth the cost of opening up, but Barnet was sure of himself. Oddly enough, it's paid off dividends, too.'

Brandon nodded as the wheels of the plane touched the beaten earth of the airstrip and bounced a couple of times. Then the plane was down and running in towards the office building.

Two men in white ducks were standing by the station wagon in front of the veranda. Trevor taxied the plane almost up to the building and switched off the engine. The two men by the station wagon strolled across towards the plane. A third man detached himself from a deck chair under the shade of the veranda and joined them as Brandon and Trevor alighted.

'Nice to see you, Brandon,' said the oldest of the men, smiling and extending his hand. He was a plump, red-faced man, perspiring from every pore. His handshake was limp.

Brandon smiled amiably. He had met Lornsby on one or two occasions before, had not taken a very great fancy to the man. However, Lornsby was quite an important person, and if he was here in Mandibarza to meet Brandon there was some good reason behind it.

Lornsby introduced his companion: a tall, stringy-looking Frenchman who had obviously spent the greater part of his life in the tropics.

'Brandon, this is M. Lecot,' said Lornsby with a wave of his hand.

The Frenchman bowed slightly. His angular face broke in an engaging smile. Brandon liked him immediately, sizing him up at a glance as a straightforward, reliable person with a sense of humour that showed itself plainly in his eyes.

The third man of the trio was already

deep in conversation with Trevor, the pilot. He was Barnet, in charge of the airstrip at Mandibarza. The entire party made their way to the welcome shade of the bungalow veranda, where Barnet supplied their needs in the form of long, cool drinks.

Conversation was confined to the weather, the heat and the flight up from the coast. Brandon contented himself with taking stock of his companions, saying little himself. He was intrigued by the presence of Lecot, though he had already had a hunch that his mysterious summons might have something to do with the uneasy international situation that faced the world. Although Lornsby had not mentioned the fact, Lecot was an extremely influential man in French Equatorial Africa. The knowledge whetted Brandon's curiosity, but it was plain that he would not learn much till the three of them were free to talk without strangers to listen.

Presently Lornsby rose to his feet.

'Well,' he said a shade pompously, 'I think we ought to be on our way, Brandon. Lots to talk about, what? Have to get organised if you're going to bring back all those wild animals!' He laughed fatly, his double chin shaking.

Brandon and Lecot rose as well. Lornsby wiped his neck and forehead with a large red handkerchief. The heat was oppressive, but Lecot seemed to have sweated out all the moisture in his body years ago. His face was dry and brown. Brandon was hot, but not so uncomfortably hot as Lornsby.

Barnet and Trevor wished them goodbye, watching as they entered the station wagon.

Lornsby himself was driving. Brandon and Lecot sat behind him. Hot air rushed in through the open windscreen as Lornsby sent the car streaking away from the airstrip and out through the cluster of huts and native dwellings of the village.

The car bucked and bounded along a narrow baked mud road leading north from Mandibarza.

Brandon said nothing till they were well clear of the village.

Lecot turned and grinned at him amusedly. 'You wonder, per'aps, M'sieu Brandon, why we ask you to visit us?' he said.

'More than once,' agreed Brandon quietly. 'Can the secret come out now?'

9

Lornsby glanced over his shoulder and nodded. 'Tell him, Lecot. It's more your story than mine.'

The Frenchman brought a packet of cigarettes from his white tunic pocket and offered one to Brandon, watching his face as he did so.

'You have heard of a man called Georg Traski?' he asked.

Brandon met his eyes. Traski? he mused. 'Yes,' he said aloud. 'Disappeared in your territory a short time before the war, didn't he? A serious loss to geological exploration.'

Lecot nodded. 'Permit me to tell you the story, M'sieu Brandon,' he said. 'It is important, you understand? Georg Traski was an alien, naturally, but an infinitely clever one, above considerations of nationality in his work.'

'So I've heard,' said Brandon. 'What really happened to him? And what was he surveying for in these parts?'

Lecot lowered his voice in a manner subconsciously dramatic.

'A very rare mineral, m'sieu,' he murmured. 'In those days he was employed by my government to locate a reef of irikum,

10

which even then had been recognised as of great energy potential from the point of view of atomic research. It has since been proved beyond doubt to be vastly superior to any other mineral used for the purpose. Uranium is as nothing compared with the value of irikum for producing atomic energy!' He spread his hands, staring at Brandon with eyebrows raised.

'Did he find irikum?'

Lecot nodded. '*Oui, oui*, m'sieu! He brought some samples from the deep interior, very rich samples. But he would not say where he had actually found them. Instead, he insisted on fitting out a second expedition before making a more detailed survey.'

Brandon nodded. 'And he never came back, is that it?'

'He did not return, m'sieu!'

Lornsby swung the station wagon through the gateway of a large bungalow set in a clearing in the forest of trees. As he brought it to a halt in front of the veranda he turned his head to Brandon.

'Georg Traski found irikum!' he stated. 'Whether he located it in French territory or not, we don't know, but the need for it has grown more urgent than ever. That's why you're here, Brandon. Western Europe wants irikum, and you're going to find it!'

Brandon said nothing in reply. His mind was going over what he'd been told, checking and remembering several things that had been left unsaid. Georg Traski was not the only man to search for the fabulous deposits of irikum reputed to be there in the vast country of forest and swamp which lay ahead. He decided to test his ground with Lornsby.

The station wagon rolled to a stop. Lornsby opened the door and waited for Brandon and Lecot to alight.

'Wasn't there someone else who disappeared more recently than Traski?' Brandon asked.

Lornsby shot him a glance that was not entirely friendly.

'Yes,' he grunted. 'Steven Shaw and his daughter were foolhardy enough to follow in Traski's footsteps. That was over a year ago. They never came back.'

Brandon grinned as the three of them made their way up the steps of the bungalow. 'So I'm to be just as much a fool, am I?' he remarked amusedly. 'I suppose you reckon I'll be different from the others? I shall return, eh?'

Lornsby grunted. He was beginning to feel very hot and very bad-tempered. That wouldn't do, he told himself.

Lecot said: 'M'sieu Brandon, none of us is a fool. We realise the dangers of what we ask you to undertake, but it is a vital matter.'

Brandon laughed softly. 'Oh, that's all right,' he said. 'I'm not complaining. But you must admit that this irikum seems to have a fatal effect on the people who look for it. Seekers die, in fact!'

'But you will not die, m'sieu,' said Lecot firmly. 'We hear stories about you, yes? You are a useful man. If you can find Traski's source of irikum it will do a great deal to stabilise security in our troubled times. You will gain the admiration and respect of every member nation of Western Union. Nor will the reward stop at that, *mon ami!*'

Brandon sank into a wicker chair on the veranda, looking from one to the other of his two companions.

'When I agreed to come here I was ready

to take on the job for you, gentlemen. I'm still ready, but aren't I right in saying that George Traski disappeared in the equatorial forest land further south of here? Doctor Shaw and his daughter, too …?'

Lecot nodded quickly. 'We chose Mandibarza for a meeting because it will allay any suspicion,' he answered. 'You will prepare your safari party further south — in the Cameroons to be precise. Most of it is arranged already.' He broke off, smiling. 'You see, m'sieu, we guessed you would be ready to give your services in the interests of peace.'

Brandon grinned despite himself. 'All right,' he said.

2

The Man with the Gramophone

Brandon remained at the bungalow with Lornsby and Lecot for three days. During that time he learnt all there was to know about the previous expeditions that had sought for irikum. Georg Traski, a queer, close-mouthed foreigner, had certainly found what he set out to find. But his secret had died with him. The authorities knew roughly the district he had penetrated; but that was all. No trace of the man or his party had ever been found.

As for Doctor Steven Shaw and his daughter, Coralie, they had gone into the swampy forests with a well-equipped safari. Many attempts had been made to find them, but none had been successful. It was assumed that some disaster had overtaken them and wiped out the entire party. Such a thing was by no means impossible in the kind of territory into which they had ventured.

Now Brandon, geologist and big game hunter, was prepared to set out. At the end of his three-day stay with Lornsby and the Frenchman he was flown to a remote village on the French bank of the upper Sanga River. This was the stepping off place which had previously served both Traski and Doctor Shaw.

Brandon was ready for the arrangements already made for him by Lornsby and Lecot. On arrival he discovered that a white man living there had put in considerable effort in getting most of the preliminary work well organised.

'You'll have thirty of the best men in the district,' said Morton, his new acquaintance. 'Hand-picked! And yesterday the Frenchies sent five trucks up river. They're being checked over now. If you don't have a successful hunting trip after all the trouble we've taken you ought to be ashamed of yourself!'

They laughed together, Brandon wondering if Morton was in on the secret or not. However, he wasn't taking any chances. Morton gave him passes signed by the French Government authorities. They were hunting permits for use in the territory through which he expected to pass. No one would ask to see them, of course, but the legal side must be attended to. Morton had done it well.

After a week more of preparation, during which time Brandon's guns and personal equipment were flown on from Lagos, the safari was almost ready to leave.

Morton and Brandon were sipping an evening drink on the veranda of the bungalow. Fires were glowing in the village and mosquitos pinged monotonously in the shadow of the baobab trees nearby.

'One more day ought to see you off,' said Morton quietly. 'Are you satisfied with everything, old man?'

Brandon nodded. He lounged backwards, relaxed and almost cool. 'My best find to date has been N'gambi,' he said.

'You certainly were darned lucky running on him!' agreed Morton. 'He's the best around here when it comes to handling the men.'

Brandon nodded again. He was far more intrigued by the fact that N'gambi had acted as guide and headman for the first part of Georg Traski's ill-fated second expedition. This information he kept to himself.

Brandon decided he would take N'gambi into his confidence only when they were well on their way. In the meantime he fobbed him off with a story that he was after gorillas.

N'gambi had nodded, but grinned as though he understood there was more to their expedition than Brandon was letting on. Brandon smiled to himself as he remembered the scene. Then Morton broke in on his thoughts again: 'Funny you setting off from this God-forsaken spot,' he remarked. 'It's an unlucky starting point in my opinion.'

Brandon glanced at him in the deepening gloom of the swift-falling tropical night. All around them was noise, from the village, from the trees, even from the ground itself, little rustling sounds that had no meaning in themselves but were part of the immense African night.

'Unlucky, is it?' he murmured. 'Don't let my men hear you say that!'

Morton laughed softly. 'I was only

thinking of poor old Shaw and his daughter,' he said. 'Coralie, that was her name. One of the loveliest girls I've ever seen, by heaven!'

'It doesn't do to brood on things like that,' observed Brandon, rising to his feet and standing with his back to Morton, staring out from the veranda towards the bright sparks of fires in the village. Shadowy figures, copper-tinted where the flames were reflected on their dark skins, moved about in the fire-shot darkness. The wailing song of a native woman reached his ears, another part of night.

'Who's brooding now?' asked Morton from behind him.

Brandon turned. 'Thanks,' he said.

In the cool hours of the following morning he strode down to where the trucks were being loaded with equipment. He was taking with him rifles and shotguns for every type of game that was likely to be met with. Not only would he probably use them, but to bolster up his story of a hunting trip it was as well to show off all the props he could.

Standing by the foremost of the five

trucks was N'gambi, a checking list of stores in his hand. He wore a pair of stained khaki shorts and an ancient panama hat. His face was gleaming in the early sunlight. At sight of Brandon he shouted to his men and then turned to his latest employer.

'Nearly finished now,' he said.

Brandon nodded. 'Good,' he said. 'I want to get away at dawn tomorrow.'

N'gambi nodded. Brandon was told that the fuel truck was being loaded now. That would be the last. N'gambi himself was checking everything. Even so, Brandon decided to go round with him, preferring to have two sets of eyes on everything. Even experienced men like N'gambi could make mistakes, as he knew to his cost from past experience.

They toiled all through the heat of the day. It was gruelling work, but when at length it was finished, Brandon had the satisfaction of knowing that nothing had been forgotten, nothing damaged or misplaced in the packing. They were likely to be cut off from civilisation for several months, so it was as well to take every precaution he could before starting.

That evening when he and Morton were relaxing over a meal in the lounge of the bungalow they both glanced up sharply at the unexpected sound of a motor engine breaking in on the other sounds that filled the air.

'Visitors?' murmured Morton blankly, 'I wasn't expecting any, were you?'

Brandon shook his head. 'No,' he replied.

The lights of a car swept round the front of the house and came to a stop, shining straight into their eyes as they rose from their seats. The engine, a noisy one, was turned off suddenly but the headlights were left full on.

From behind their glare a figure appeared, hurrying up the steps of the veranda. It was a small figure, that of a narrow-shouldered man.

'Hello, there,' said Morton.

'Oh, yes ... Good evening, gentlemen.' Seen clearly for the first time, their unexpected visitor was a somewhat curious spectacle. Middle-aged, with thin hair that was almost white, he gave an impression of untidiness. His suit of ducks was crumpled and none too clean. The sleeves of his jacket were several inches too short for him.

Brandon noticed that he was forever tugging them down towards his wrists in a vain attempt to free his elbows.

'Good evening,' said Brandon. 'Won't you tell us who you are?' He glanced at Morton obliquely, grinning despite his curiosity.

'Oh ... ah — yes. My name's Betts, Arthur Betts,' the newcomer informed them. 'I was looking for Mr. Rex Brandon, who I believe is somewhere in this village. I — er, that is it's rather important, really. Most definitely important, you know.'

'It probably is,' said Brandon soothingly. 'I'm the man you're looking for. What can I do for you? Come on in and have a drink.'

'Never touch it, sir; never touch it!' averred Arthur Betts firmly. 'Mr. Brandon, I'm delighted to meet you!' He thrust out a thin, sinewy hand and grasped Brandon's tightly.

Morton looked on with a wrinkle of amusement on his face.

'Come along in,' he said, butting in loudly. Still grasping Brandon's arm, Betts permitted himself to be drawn inside the bungalow.

'Is it true that you're leaving in the morning on a big game hunt in the interior?' he demanded urgently when they were gathered in the main room, with Morton pouring drinks for himself and Brandon.

Brandon eyed him guardedly. Then: 'Yes,' he admitted. 'But tell me, where did you spring from, Mr. Betts?'

'Oh, me …? Yes, well I'm a zoologist, and I wondered if you could possibly take me along with you when you go from here. You see, sir, it's really important!' His eyes were bright behind rimless glasses that clung to his long, pointed nose precariously. 'Really important,' he repeated.

Brandon was non-committal. He did not want anyone else with him, but at the same time he felt it would be wise to find out what lay behind this last-minute arrival.

'I'm a zoologist,' Betts told him again. 'I've heard there's a very rare example of gorilla in the jungle for which you're making. If you'll let me come with you I shall have an opportunity of studying its habits.' His eyes were pleading with Brandon now, almost desperately it seemed. This was certainly an important thing to Betts.

Brandon was on the point of refusing as politely as he could when Morton interposed, urging him to make room for the visitor. 'After all,' he said reasonably enough, 'it isn't as if you're tied in any way.'

Brandon shot him a look, before remembering that Morton did not know of any ulterior purposes behind the safari. He turned to Betts again.

'How did you know I was going on safari?' he asked.

'Loango!' replied the little man quickly. 'There is talk down there, on the coast, of Rex Brandon starting another hunting trip.'

Brandon raised his eyebrows slightly. 'To the forest where your pet gorillas live ...?'

Betts fluttered his hands. 'I guessed you would make for that district,' he said, a little too hurriedly. 'If you are after game worth getting you would be bound to enter Borwingi territory. A foregone conclusion, if I may say so.'

Brandon hesitated. He was beginning to like Betts, in spite of certain misgivings. The little man must have driven all the way to the village from Loango. It was not a bad feat, and there was no denying the man's enthusiasm.

'Got your gear?' he asked quietly.

Betts gave a tremendous sigh of relief, shutting his eyes for an instant.

'You'll take me with you?' he countered breathlessly.

'I haven't said so yet. What kit have you got? My trucks are pretty well loaded down as it is.'

Betts turned on his heel and almost ran from the room, out to his car.

Brandon and Morton exchanged glances and grinned.

'Odd little cove,' remarked Morton.

'Very,' said Brandon thoughtfully. 'Oh well, I suppose I shan't lose anything by taking him with me. He might be quite amusing, in fact.'

Betts returned before either of them could say anything further.

'I have my luggage with me,' he announced. 'I am ready to leave with you whenever you say the word. See!'

Brandon put a hand to his mouth. Betts was standing in the open doorway with a butterfly net and fishing rod in one hand,

and a portable gramophone case in the other. His face was wreathed in smiles, and he blinked rapidly as he peered through his rimless spectacles at his hosts.

'Very well,' said Brandon rather helplessly. 'Dump it somewhere. We leave at dawn for … unknown parts.'

3

Omens of Trouble

Morton looked at Brandon with a speculative eye. Then he sent for one of Brandon's manservants and gave orders for a room to be prepared for the visitor.

Arthur Betts was as eager as a schoolboy once he knew for sure that he was to accompany Brandon on safari. He told them he considered it a great honour, and went on to say that he had definite hopes of locating the rare variety of gorilla that rumour insisted was to be found in Borwingi country.

Brandon found himself absorbing a certain amount of the little zoologist's enthusiasm, but at the same time he was beginning to wonder about the man on a number of other scores.

Was Betts after nothing less innocent than zoological knowledge? Brandon decided to keep a pretty close eye on his companion. It was always possible that Betts was a far more clever man than he gave him credit for being. And in view of the real objectives behind the safari, it was important to make quite sure.

Through a series of carefully phrased questions, Brandon soon discovered that Betts was undoubtedly a zoologist, as he claimed. A few more questions, which in themselves gave nothing away, confirmed Brandon's amicable feelings towards Betts. The man knew several acquaintances of Brandon's, both in Africa and in other parts of the world, which he seemed to have travelled extensively during his life.

Satisfied, Brandon turned in that night with a sense of restlessness such as always assailed him before the start of a trip. He knew that no matter how many times he set off to penetrate the almost unexplored part of the world, he would always experience that feeling.

He still felt that Betts was something of a mystery, but he did not now think that the man was intending to cause any trouble. If he was wrong, time would prove it. Meanwhile, he was content to leave things as they were, keeping his wits about him for any adverse signs.

Betts left his car — a rather decrepit vehicle — in Morton's care. When the safari started a few minutes before the sun topped the trees Betts was travelling in the rear truck, that which carried the fuel stores for the party. Brandon himself was driving the leading vehicle, with N'gambi in the cab alongside him. The other trucks were driven by local men who had served in the Forces during the war and were proficient at their job.

Betts had his gramophone with him. Whether it worked or not, Brandon was still to learn. He wondered idly what sort of selection of records the odd little man carried. A few miles outside the village the country changed from thickly growing trees and scrub to more open terrain. So far there had been a road of sorts for the trucks, but once the trees thinned this road gradually vanished. Brandon led the convoy through a belt of tall savanna grass which rose almost to the top of the leading vehicle's radiator. The speed was naturally slow; with limited visibility, N'gambi had to stand on the running board and shout out warnings if the ground became too uneven.

However, by noon they had covered a considerable distance. Brandon threw out the clutch and brought the truck to a standstill in the welcome shade of a low baobab tree. Scrub and acacia grew thickly all round, forming a natural island in the sea of savanna grass. The other vehicles drew up in a rough semi-circle, their drivers clambering down. The rest of the bearers dropped to the ground, chatting among themselves and glancing at N'gambi for orders. Until the going became difficult the main number of bearers were merely passengers, but Brandon knew that a time would come when they would have to hack a path through dense undergrowth, or even carry the stores on their backs if things went wrong. There were many places where the trucks would be useless, and might even have to be abandoned.

Betts alighted from the last of the vehicles, coming across to join Brandon where he stood beside his truck as N'gambi gave orders for the preparation of a meal. Bearers hastily set up an awning against the intense heat, while others unloaded the petrol stoves.

'Well, Arthur!' said Brandon, grinning. 'Is this what you wanted?'

Betts blinked behind the lenses of his glasses. His face was serious, but the angle at which he wore his topee was almost ludicrous. Brandon was forced to smile.

'There is very little game about for you to shoot,' said Betts thoughtfully. 'I can't understand it. There should be plenty in this vicinity.'

Brandon nodded. He, too, had noticed the scarcity of wild life in the section through which they had travelled. However, there were any number of possible reasons for that and he gave it only a passing thought.

Shortly afterwards they were sitting down to a meal in the scant protection of the awning.

Leaning back when it was over, Rex Brandon felt for his pipe and filled it carefully, his long brown fingers moving deliberately as he pressed the tobacco down in its bowl.

Betts turned and opened his gramophone case, which one of the bearers had brought from the truck. While Brandon was busy with his pipe, the zoologist started the music.

Brandon glanced up with a smile of amusement as the first bars of 'Trees' drifted out from the gramophone.

Betts looked up and smiled at him.

'You like it?' he asked. 'It's the only tune there is, as far as I'm concerned. A wonderful piece!'

Brandon nodded wordlessly. Surely, he thought, Betts was not going to play 'Trees' every time they stopped?

'Have you any other records?' he inquired.

Betts shook his head firmly. 'None,' he replied.

'Oh,' murmured Brandon. 'Never mind.'

Betts hummed contentedly in time with the gramophone. Brandon made an effort and succeeded in looking on the bright side. He liked Betts as a man, and must make allowances, he thought. But only one tune ... !

They broke camp and continued on their way, pressing on across the plain of savanna grass and low-growing scrub. In the far distance, Brandon sighted the dark green hump of forest-clad hills. At about the same time he had his first glimpse of game. Streaking over the ground away to the north was a herd of antelope, light and graceful as the wind as they disappeared, frightened by the rumble of the trucks.

That evening when they halted for the night all was quiet. He and Betts watched their men as they sat round the fire, singing their own songs.

'By tomorrow or the next day we shall reach the fringe of the Borwingi country,' observed Brandon.

Betts nodded, winding his gramophone thoughtfully.

Brandon sighed, but said nothing more. When he turned into his tent and closed the mosquito net over and round his safari bed he could still hear the music of 'Trees' being ground out from the direction of Betts' tent a few yards away. In desperation he drew the sheet over his head and hoped for the best.

The days wore on uneventfully enough. Both men bagged a small amount of game for the pot, but the big stuff was yet to come. Betts, an indifferent shot, was full of open admiration for the marksmanship of Brandon, who could bring down a running animal at very long range. The deeper they penetrated into the Borwingi territory the more plentiful was game, and on several occasions Brandon and N'gambi found the spoor of lions, leopards, giraffe and rhinoceros. But Brandon did not spend much time in hunting the various creatures. He was eager now to press on into the country where Georg Traski had disappeared.

Calling N'gambi aside when camp had been made one night, he took him some distance from the tents and fires under the pretence of examining some tracks in the ground, which was marshy here.

'I see no tracks,' murmured N'gambi presently.

'You won't,' replied Brandon with a grin. 'I want to talk to you about some other tracks. A white man's tracks.'

N'gambi eyed him shrewdly. 'Yes?' he answered.

'You acted as guide and headman to Georg Traski some years ago,' said Brandon slowly. 'I know these things, N'gambi. Now I want to go where Traski went, for I seek the things he sought.'

N'gambi nodded. 'It is true, what you say, *bwana*,' he replied. 'But there is much danger; that I know. And I cannot take you all the way in the white man's footsteps, for I left him before the end of his safari.'

'Never mind,' said Brandon. 'Will you guide me as far as you can?'

'Yes.'

'And say nothing of what I have spoken to your fellows.'

'It is understood. You are hunting.'

'I am hunting,' said Brandon with a nod. 'But you and I know we are not after game only. Mr. Betts does not, though, so do not tell him.'

N'gambi ducked his head quickly in answer.

'Let us return to camp, N'gambi. It is well that we talk.'

N'gambi detained him with a gesture. 'I, too, have words to speak,' he said.

Brandon waited, wondering what was coming.

N'gambi said: 'The bearers are growing

uneasy. I think you should know that.'

Brandon's forehead creased in a frown. He looked at N'gambi inquiringly.

'Borwingi country is bad,' said N'gambi quietly. 'The rest, they do not like it. And they say safari not a good one. I hope we have no bad luck or there may be trouble.'

'I see,' answered Brandon slowly. 'You'll have to keep an eye on 'em, N'gambi. This safari is more important than a hunting trip.'

N'gambi nodded. 'It shall be done.'

Brandon was thoughtful when he got back to camp. He said nothing to Betts about the information given him. Betts was probably just as innocent as he appeared on the surface, but it was a remote possibility that he might be stirring up rumours among the men. He determined to take no chances.

For the next three days progress was easier. Then they were entering the fringe of the bush that edged the deeper forests of acacia and baobab that covered the rising hills. Trailing lianas hindered them. The men had to leave the trucks and hack a path for the vehicles. Myriad brightly coloured birds chattered and swooped from branch to branch above their heads. Betts grew very excited when he caught sight of a small, wrinkle-faced monkey which he said was quite a rarity in these parts.

Night found them camped in a small clearing. Brandon would have carried on further that day had it not been for the fact that one of the trucks was giving trouble. Ozozam, the driver, seemed uneasy about it. According to him, the engine had started to overheat almost as soon as they had set off that morning. By the noon halt it was boiling all the time. Obviously something would have to be done about it. Brandon put N'gambi on to stripping the cooling system down while he and Betts went out with the guns after game. When they returned to camp it was to find that the water pump was broken and the truck was unusable.

The news caused Brandon to frown. He gave orders for the vehicle to be unloaded, then checked through the stores and decided what could safely be left behind. The remainder was loaded on to the other trucks. By that time it was too late to carry on.

Lulled to sleep by the noises of the night, Brandon lay flat on his back under the protection of his mosquito net. The men were long ago dreaming, while Betts had stopped his gramophone well over an hour previously.

Somewhere in the distance the roar of a lion broke through the other sounds of the forest. For a moment it stilled the smaller noises of the little night animals searching for food. Then they broke out again with renewed clamour.

Brandon stirred restlessly, opening his eyes and peering round in the darkness of his tent. Through the open fly he caught a glimpse of the smouldering fire, over which sat one of the bearers on guard. As Brandon watched, the shadowy figure of N'gambi crossed the clearing, halting for a moment close to the watchman and exchanging a few words before fading out again in the gloom beyond the fire.

It was then that they first heard the drums.

From what seemed a very long way off, they beat with incessant, monotonous rhythm, rising and falling as the night wind carried the sound across the tree-tops to their camp.

Brandon sat up in bed, leaning on one elbow, frowning. He realised only too well that the sound of Borwingi drums was the last thing to bolster the courage of his bearers. Already during the day he had noticed many furtive glances passing between the superstitious locals who made up his party. The breakdown of the truck had been magnified out of all proportions, until it assumed the bulk of *ju-ju* in the eyes of the men.

Were they war drums? Brandon did not think so. But he knew well enough that the coming of the party would by now have been noted and reported to the chiefs of the various Borwingi tribes in the district. None of these scouts had been spotted, but Brandon had had previous experience of the bush-telegraph in use in the wilds. No one could deny its efficiency of operation.

The figure of Arthur Betts loomed black in the tent opening.

'Hello,' he said quietly. 'You hear them, Rex?'

'Just as plainly as you do. What do you

make of it?'

Betts sat himself down on the edge of Brandon's bed. He wore a pair of gaudy pyjamas borrowed from Morton before the start of the safari. In his hand was a bottle of quinine tablets. He swallowed a couple before answering.

'Nothing much,' he said presently. 'They're talking about us, that's all. It's only natural.'

Brandon nodded, reaching out for a cigarette. Confirmed pipe smoker though he was, there were often times when he turned to cigarettes as an alternative. This was one of them. 'I think you're right,' he said slowly. 'But I'm wondering if the rest of the men will agree with us. They're getting very edgy, you know.'

'I noticed that,' admitted Betts. He spoke in an undertone as if expecting to be overheard. 'One of them in particular was talking yesterday, in my truck. It was not good talk.'

'Incitement, you mean?' Brandon sounded really worried for the first time.

Betts shrugged in the darkness. Brandon wished he could see his face clearly, but it was only a pale smudge. He leaned over and turned on a portable hand-lamp, turning it so that it shone on Betts. Betts blinked. He was nearly blind without his glasses anyway.

'Incitement?' he echoed doubtfully. 'Not exactly. Just something about it being an unlucky safari.'

'You should have told me before now!' Brandon snapped more curtly. 'We shall find ourselves with trouble on our hands unless we're careful.'

'Would the Borwingis really attack us?' asked Betts.

'I doubt it. You'd better get back to bed before the mosquitoes eat you. I'm going to sleep again.'

'Yes ... of course.' Betts hesitated. 'Er — is this N'gambi fellow reliable?'

'I should say so. Why do you ask?'

'I just wondered.' Betts rose to his feet and moved to the tent fly, ducking through awkwardly. 'See you in the morning,' he added, turning. 'Good night!'

'Good night,' answered Brandon slowly. He frowned as he spoke, then switched off the lamp and lay back against his pillow.

Arthur Betts, he thought. What exactly was Betts up to? Had he been a fool to accept the little man's apparent innocence so completely? There were aspects of it that now struck him as vaguely suspicious. It was a long time before he finally dropped off to sleep again, and when he did the distant drums were still beating their message.

4

Clawed Killer

There was an air of tension in the camp next morning, which Brandon was quick to sense. The men moved about in almost complete silence, glancing into the bush with apprehensive eyes every now and again as if expecting danger to strike at them suddenly. Even N'gambi seemed affected by the mood that assailed his fellows.

Betts was quiet and preoccupied during breakfast.

Brandon watched him surreptitiously, no longer entirely happy about his companion. Barely formed suspicions grew in his mind. He tried to thrust them aside, but they persisted; in the end he realised he would have to keep a very close check on Betts if he was to find any peace for the remainder of the journey.

Under these uneasy circumstances the party set off again, shortly after dawn.

Brandon, changing his tactics slightly, left N'gambi in charge of the leading vehicle while he himself travelled with Betts at the rear. In this way he got to know Betts considerably better than he had done previously, for, although much quieter than before, the little zoologist talked freely enough as they bumped and rattled along in the wake of the truck ahead.

But at the noon-day halt there was more trouble waiting.

Brandon strolled forward to meet an agitated N'gambi.

'What's the matter?' demanded Brandon, catching sight of the tall man's anxious expression.

'Three of the men. They were taken sick badly. It is a sign!'

Brandon's mouth tightened. 'Take me to them at once. And no talk of *ju-ju* from you, N'gambi, understand?'

N'gambi nodded, but he was by no means happy. He led Brandon to a group of men who were clustered round one of the trucks. They eyed him in silence as he approached. Inside the truck, looking very sorry for themselves, were three of the

44

sturdy bearers.

Arthur Betts joined the group at that moment, peering short-sightedly over Brandon's shoulder as the leader bent and looked at the sick men.

It took Brandon but a short time to diagnose mild food poisoning.

Turning to Betts, he said: 'They've been eating something that didn't agree with 'em. Nuisance, but there it is.'

'I'll get the medicine chest,' offered Betts. 'This won't be the first time I've acted as a doctor!'

Brandon nodded approval. 'Glad to hear it,' he said. Then to N'gambi: 'Make camp. We shall have to stop here for a while. Probably until tomorrow. Find out what these men have been eating. If they kept food from the store truck too long that could be the cause, especially tinned stuff opened and left in this heat.'

N'gambi hesitated. Then: 'You are right, but many think it is an ill omen. Coming on top of the other trouble, and the drums last night, it is bad.'

Brandon glanced round the group of men keenly. 'No more of this talk!' he said,

45

speaking in their own language. 'If white men are not afraid, you are shamed to behave in this manner.'

One of the bearers, a tall, saturnine man, older than most of his fellows, stepped forward boldly. 'The white men are sometimes not wise.'

Brandon recognised the man as Tulani. He had already had suspicions of him. If anyone was stirring the men up with talk of *ju-ju* it would be Tulani.

'Those are bold words, Tulani,' said Brandon quietly.

'We are bold men to risk our lives in Borwingi country,' answered the man, reasonably.

'We are not taking war to the tribes of Borwingi!' said Brandon. 'Let there be no more of this talk, Tulani. If there is trouble, I shall punish the man who makes it. If your lives are in danger, I shall protect you. If my hunting is successful there will be a greater reward for those who are loyal to me.'

Tulani muttered something and made to turn away, then swung round again to face Brandon.

'This is bad safari!' he said quickly.

46

Brandon ignored the remark, beckoning N'gambi to him.

'Get everyone working and keep them busy,' he ordered curtly. 'They mustn't have time to think. Have the sick men made easy in one of the trucks. Mr. Betts will bring them medicine. Theirs is a sickness of the belly, not the mind.'

N'gambi nodded silently. In a moment or two he was lashing his men with his tongue in no uncertain manner. Even Tulani, still a little defiant, did as he was told with a speed that brought a smile to Brandon's lips as he watched.

Betts was soon on the scene, attending to the sick with remarkable efficiency. Betts was something of an enigma, thought Brandon.

He did not leave the vicinity of the camp that day, but sent Betts off with a rifle and shotgun to see what he could bag in the way of game. With Betts he sent one of the more level-headed of the men. The two returned as evening was falling.

'We saw some fresh lion spoor,' said Betts. 'Nothing else though. I missed a buck, much to Timpas' disgust!' He grinned one-sidedly.

Night had barely fallen when the music of 'Trees' was almost drowned by the throb of distant drums.

Brandon sighed deeply, cursing the drums and guessing that tomorrow there would be more uneasiness than ever in the camp.

At long last he dozed off.

Sudden bedlam brought him wide awake in an instant. The whispering night was full of noise now. From far away came the message of the drums. Closer at hand the scream of some nocturnal creatures. But right in the camp itself was the loudest and most terrifying sound of all.

The deep-throated roar of a lion jarred Brandon to full wakefulness.

Without a moment's loss of time he sprang out of bed, whipped his mosquito net aside and reached the tent fly in a single bound, stopping only to seize a high-velocity rifle as he passed.

The first thing he saw was Arthur Betts standing in the entrance of the other tent, a gun in his hand as he peered about in a confused fashion.

48

'Lion!' yelled Brandon above the din. Beyond the glow of the camp fire he saw a tawny shape, heard the scream of a man in mortal fear. Leaping forward, he was horrified to see a great, dark-maned monster disappearing in the gloom. Gripped between its jaws was one of the men, being dragged off to his death in the bush by the yellow king of the jungle.

The lion and its burden, still screaming, had vanished from sight beyond the fire. Brandon could hear the crash of foliage and thorn scrub being brushed aside as the lion retreated.

He shouted for N'gambi, then darted forward in the wake of the lion. Betts thumped along behind Brandon, shouting out something about thorns. Brandon did not heed him. He knew that unless he was very fortunate, the lion would have killed the man by the time he could get a shot at the night marauder.

The bush outside the camp thickened so that they were forced to break their way through. Thorns tore at their pyjamas. Brandon cursed as he trod heavily on a sharp piece of branch. Turning for a glimpse of Betts, he found his companion had disappeared. Pausing for an instant, he listened. Somewhere ahead, the worrying sound of the lion came loudly. He'd be too late to save the man.

Taking more care now, he carried on, following the broken trail of the animal. The bush was suddenly quiet, as if every creature in range had frozen into immobility at the challenging roar of the lion. Then a little clearing opened up ahead of him. Brandon halted abruptly, staring through the darkness at the hideous scene before him.

The lion was crouched over a dark form on the ground. There were no longer any screams or cries from the bearer. Brandon raised his rifle to his shoulder, lining up the luminous bead of the sight on a point just behind the animal's shoulder. The lion scented him at the same moment as he squeezed the trigger. With a tremendous leap it hurled its sinewy body forward. The sudden crack of the rifle and the creature's roar were almost simultaneous. Brandon leapt aside as the tawny body crashed into the thorn scrub close beside him.

Almost in the same instant a second rifle

spoke from the other side of the clearing. Brandon actually felt the fan of wind as the steel-coated bullet ripped through the air only inches from his head. He cursed and gave the lion another shot, killing it immediately.

Arthur Betts broke into view from nearby scrub as Brandon raised his head.

'You damned fool!' snapped Brandon. 'What do you think you're doing, man? That last shot nearly had me!'

Betts blinked at him vacantly. Somewhere in the bush he'd lost his glasses. Brandon, angry with him and full of renewed suspicion, seized his rifle and snapped the bolt back. An unfired cartridge rattled out as the ejector clicked.

Before he could speak again, N'gambi and several of the men appeared, N'gambi with an electric lamp in his hand.

Betts and Brandon stared at each other for a second or two, neither man speaking. Then the frantic words of the men brought their heads round.

Brandon found it difficult to concentrate on what N'gambi was saying. The unfortunate bearer was dead when they picked him

51

up. Brandon's first shot had struck the lion in the chest. His second one, at close range, had passed through its skull to its brain.

'Return,' urged N'gambi. 'You are torn and bleeding from the thorns. They are dangerous.'

Brandon nodded wordlessly. His brain was in a whirl. He and Betts exchanged a glance. If Betts hadn't fired that second shot from the darkness, who had? Brandon knew it would be useless trying to find out before morning. If there was an unknown killer at large in the forest of scrub and thorn, it would require plenty of light to track him. But could Betts have had anything to do with it at all?

He was still pondering the question as he made his way back to camp with the odd little zoologist beside him.

The rest of the men brought up the rear, carrying the badly mauled body of their comrade. Tulani was bewailing the fact that no one had listened to his warnings. N'gambi ordered him to be silent, but already Tulani was beginning to influence his fellow bearers.

5

Where There's Smoke ...

'Come into my tent,' said Betts very quietly as they limped back into the camp. 'I'll dress these thorn scratches with antiseptic.'

Brandon grunted. He waited until they were inside the tent before speaking. Then, as Betts opened the medicine chest and busied himself with bottles, he sat on a canvas chair and studied the man narrowly.

'What do you know about that shot that was fired?' he asked a moment later.

Betts raised his head. He was wearing his spare pair of spectacles now. In ragged pyjamas now spattered with blood he cut a grotesque figure, his thin face outlined in the up-thrown glare of the electric lamp by which he was working. Brandon thought he caught a hint of something like fear in his gaze as Betts turned towards him. He might have been wrong.

'You thought I fired it, didn't you?' said

Betts a shade truculently. His tone surprised Brandon.

'A natural enough assumption,' he answered. 'What do you know about it, Arthur?'

Betts didn't speak for a moment, but instead came across and started dabbing the scratches on Brandon's arms. Then: 'I was under the impression that you'd done all the shooting,' he murmured.

Brandon hesitated. 'I didn't,' he replied. 'Some other person took a deliberate shot at me. He must have fired at the flash of my first shot. If I hadn't jumped out of the lion's way when it sprang, he'd have got me, too.'

Betts examined his arm thoughtfully, head bent. Without meeting Brandon's eyes he said: 'I'm none too happy about this trip of ours. There's something odd about it.'

'Is there?' Brandon's voice was edged when he spoke. 'I hadn't noticed it myself.'

'I have.'

'No one asked you to come with me!' Brandon felt his temper being frayed by Betts' mild manner.

'I admit that. If you like I'll start back in

the morning.'

'Don't be a fool!' snorted Brandon. 'Sorry, but I don't like being shot at in the dark.'

Betts stood up straight and looked him squarely in the eye for the first time. 'Why can't you be frank with me?' he said. 'You're not out in the wilds like this just for the sake of a few hunting trophies. You're a geologist, first and foremost. And you're not the only geologist to come to these parts, either.'

Brandon rose to his feet very slowly. 'Look, Arthur,' he said carefully, 'we're both a little overwrought. I'd be glad if we could leave this discussion until morning. There are several points I want to think about before we go any further. For one thing, I'm certain that *someone* tried to kill me a little while ago. Assuming that it wasn't you, there's a possibility that one of the other men had a shot at it. From now on I suggest we both watch our step.'

Betts smiled at that. 'All right,' he said slowly. 'I'm glad we're not going to quarrel.' He hesitated, then looked up impulsively. 'If there's anything I can do to help, you've only got to say so. I'm still here for my own purposes, Rex, but there isn't any reason why they shouldn't run parallel to yours.'

Brandon forced a grin to his face. 'Thanks,' he said. 'Tomorrow morning I'm going over the ground beyond the camp with a fine-toothed comb. Someone used a rifle last night and they must have left tracks.'

Betts nodded. Without another word he finished dabbing Brandon's wounds with antiseptic lotion. Then Brandon did the same for Betts. Neither man said anything more on the subject that had come up between them; but Brandon felt a certain sense of relief as he made his way back to his own tent. His suspicions regarding Betts were more or less allayed. If his findings when he looked over the ground in the morning were what he hoped they would be, the zoologist could be cleared.

Reaching his own tent he paused in the entrance. The night was still oppressively hot and steamy. A large yellow moon was creeping up from behind the trees. In the gloom Brandon saw several groups of his men talking quietly. The situation was by no means a pleasant one. This latest disaster would do more to unnerve the already edgy men than anything else could have done. It was just one thing after another. Nor did the almost incessant beat of the drums quiet his fears.

Up again before dawn, he summoned N'gambi to his tent. Betts was also present at the conference.

When N'gambi appeared, Brandon asked him to sit down and listen. N'gambi had left the rest of the men doing work of one kind and another. Anything, Brandon had told him, that would keep their minds occupied. On Brandon's suggestion, too, N'gambi had dispatched Tulani and another man to the clearing where the lion had been killed. Brandon thought it better to keep the troublemaker out of the way as much as he could.

'N'gambi,' he began, 'what I tell you now you must keep to yourself. It is important, you understand?'

N'gambi gave a nod. He sat stiffly on the canvas chair with his battered panama hat perched on his left knee, strong fingers gripping the limp brim.

'When I hunted the lion last night, some

unknown man took a shot at me, N'gambi. It was only luck that saved me.'

N'gambi looked startled for an instant, then worried.

'But who would try to kill you, *bwana*?' he asked.

'That's what you and I are going to find out,' answered Brandon grimly. 'You are a good tracker, aren't you?'

The headman nodded again. 'It has been said so in the past,' he admitted with a touch of pride in his voice. 'I will do my best.'

'Let it be known that we are going out to find the place where the lion came from,' said Brandon. 'It may have left a mate or cubs behind, which will be dangerous. Tell everyone that.'

'But we go after another sort of game, yes?'

'Yes!' Brandon nodded firmly. 'Game that can use a rifle, N'gambi. I don't know where it comes from, but we can't afford to leave it loose. Be ready to leave in ten minutes' time. No word of this, remember.'

'It is understood.' N'gambi rose and stood stiffly in front of Brandon. Then he turned and left the tent.

Betts glanced at Brandon curiously. 'Is it wise to trust N'gambi so completely?'

Brandon grinned and shrugged. 'He's a first-class tracker,' he said. 'And I think he can be trusted. If I'm wrong, then there's certainly no one else I can trust in this outfit.'

Betts gave a grunt and went on working methodically. He was bathing a nasty thorn gash.

'I am still anxious to find one of those gorillas I've heard about,' he said presently. 'What would you do if the men gave real trouble?'

Brandon hesitated for a brief moment only. Then: 'Carry on according to plan,' he said quietly. 'I'm not in the habit of turning back once I start something.'

'Good!' remarked Betts in a satisfied tone. 'You can count on me if you want to.'

'There mustn't be any real trouble,' said Brandon firmly. 'We don't want it unless it's forced on us.'

'There you are,' said Betts, straightening up. 'Now you can go. Those thorns certainly left their mark on us!'

'Thanks. I'll be off with N'gambi now.

Now look, Arthur, I'm leaving you in charge of the camp. Tulani is out skinning the lion, so you won't have him to cope with, but keep an eye on the rest. We'll be back about noon, I hope. Keep the men as busy as you can. Get the trucks cleaned and maintained. And don't forget those three we have sick. If there's any trouble, fire that signal pistol a couple of times.'

Betts nodded gravely. 'You can rely on me,' he said. 'I shan't let you down.'

Brandon clapped him on the shoulder. Although Betts was considerably older than himself, Brandon always felt a sense of being with someone whose enthusiasm would have put a youth to shame. Enthusiasm and earnestness were Betts' strong points.

Outside the tent, Brandon found N'gambi waiting for him with the rifles and haversacks of food.

Under the curious, vaguely distrustful glances of the men, the two of them left the camp and disappeared into the bush.

'Keep going as we are for a while,' said Brandon. 'Then we'll back-track. I want to examine the ground all around the camp.

That shot last night was no stray!'

N'gambi nodded. They were nearing the spot where Brandon had killed the lion. Faintly on the breeze, they could hear the voices of Tulani and his companion as they worked on the carcase where it lay at the edge of the scrub.

Brandon halted and turned off at right angles to their line of progress. In a big sweep, moving slowly and quietly, they worked right round the camp site at a distance of roughly a hundred yards. N'gambi, head bent, examined the ground minutely as he walked. Sometimes he bent on one knee and almost sniffed the earth, only to shake his head and rise.

But at length he looked at Brandon excitedly, pointing to a series of faint marks in the soft earth near the roots of a low-growing acacia tree just within sight of the camp.

'A man stand here!' he announced. 'See, he wears boots. The prints of his feet are deeper where he stood still and watched.' He glanced through the curtain of tree and thorn growth in the direction of the camp. The trucks and tents were plainly visible.

61

Brandon frowned, puzzled by what he saw. Then he turned to N'gambi. 'This is as far as he came?' he asked.

The tall black nodded, then started to cast around for further sign. When he found it Brandon saw that the unknown man had approached the camp from a more or less northerly direction. The shot had been fired near the place where the lion had died, which lay more to the west of where they were now.

With N'gambi's expert guidance and tracking skills they followed a faintly discernible line taken by the stranger to the clearing. Checking carefully, Brandon made sure that the line of footprints did not touch or cross those of Betts or himself, but followed a parallel course.

By the time they reached the clearing, Tulani and his fellow bearer had completed the task of skinning the lion and returned to camp. They had the scene to themselves.

It did not take N'gambi long to locate the spot from which the treacherous shot had been fired at Brandon in the night.

N'gambi indicated a depression where the man had been standing at the time.

Then he bent swiftly and picked something up from where it had fallen a few feet away. Holding it out in silence, he left Brandon white leader to draw his own conclusions.

Brandon took the expended cartridge case and examined it thoughtfully.

'A .300 military cartridge,' he mused slowly. 'We haven't got a weapon in the outfit that takes these shells.'

'Then it was not one of us who fired at you.' N'gambi's simple and undeniable logic brought a grim smile to Brandon's lips.

'No,' he replied. 'I think we can accept that as true. The next thing we have to discover is where the man went.'

'This will not be a difficult task,' he replied. 'See, after shooting at you, he retreated in a hurry, making much broken sign among the bush.'

Brandon nodded. He'd been working out the sequence in his head. This unknown man, armed with a powerful rifle, must have crept up on the camp about nightfall. He had stood and watched it for some considerable time. Then, when the lion had struck and dragged off his hapless victim, he had waited till Brandon and Betts set out in pursuit. The path he had taken was parallel to that of Betts. After his abortive attempt to kill Brandon he had beaten a hasty retreat.

'Come on,' said Brandon firmly. Before starting out he had taken the precaution of strapping on a revolver holster. Now he drew the weapon as he and N'gambi began to follow the easily readable tracks of a running man.

Presently the footprints, clear in the soft earth over which they went, showed that the man had slowed to a walk.

'Wait!' said Brandon. 'For all we know he may be lying up somewhere close. The scrub's getting thicker. This is devil's own country for a man-hunt!' He looked up and away to the climbing, forest-clad hills in front. The tracks of the unknown man veered away down a slope to a deep dank valley. From where they were they could see the mist of damp vegetation as it steamed in the growing heat of day.

'It is well we move slowly,' murmured N'gambi. 'In Borwingi country anything happens!' He looked warily about him.

Then suddenly his fingers closed tightly on Brandon's wrist.

Brandon turned and stared in the direction of the man's pointing arm. The chill touch of foreboding crept over him at what he saw. Rising almost straight into the air above the tree tops was a thick column of black, oily smoke. It hung there, spreading out in a vast mushroom as the upper air stirred it slightly.

'The camp!' gasped Brandon in sudden alarm. 'That's oil or petrol smoke, N'gambi!'

6

The Secret of the Swamp

Tough and hardened to travel under any conditions as he was, Rex Brandon found the going exhausting as he and N'gambi hurried back along the path they had taken. Torn and scratched, yet unheeding of the obstacles that cluttered their way, they raced for the camp as fast as they could.

But the scene that met their horrified gaze when they came within sight of the camp brought them both to an involuntary halt as they topped a rise and stared down the hill through a network of foliage.

Swearing softly, Brandon stumbled forward again.

There was now no doubt about the source of the smoke. It hung in a great pall above the site of the camp, stinging his eyes as he blundered down towards the open space beneath the baobab trees. Red hot and still burning angrily, the wreck of the fuel store lorry stood alone; there were no other trucks to keep it company. Nor was there a single one of the bearers in sight.

Brandon reached the clearing and halted, one arm thrown up against the intense heat that welled out at him from the blazing petrol and oil truck. The short grass and bush all round it were smouldering and smoking. Small pools of burning oil told of an explosion that had scattered the fuel far and wide.

N'gambi came up beside his employer, speechless as he looked on the scene of disaster that confronted them.

Then Brandon gave a sudden start and dashed forward to the very edge of the smouldering ring of grass and scrub. On the ground, blackened by heat and smoke, was the immobile figure of Arthur Betts.

Battling through the sickly fumes of the blazing oil, Brandon reached him, not knowing whether he was dead or alive, but conscious only of the urgency of getting him clear of the encroaching heat and creeping flames.

Between them, he and N'gambi dragged Betts to windward of the fire. They found a spot that was partly sheltered from the fierce heat. Lowering Betts to the ground, Brandon knelt and examined him. With a sigh of relief he looked up at N'gambi and nodded wordlessly. 'He is alive?' queried N'gambi.

Brandon nodded again. 'Yes,' he replied. 'There's a lump on the back of his head the size of an egg. Something must have hit him when the truck caught light.'

'Or some *one, bwana,*' murmured his companion.

Brandon looked up sharply. 'I hadn't thought of that,' he said grimly. 'See if you can find out where the rest of the men took the other wagons. They probably moved them out of range of the fire.'

But N'gambi shook his head. 'I do not think so. I do not think we shall see the trucks or the stores again.'

Brandon sat back on his heels for an instant as the news sank in. N'gambi was probably right. He realised that, yet still fought against the notion that they were stranded in the forest country of the Borwingi without stores or vehicles, with Betts hurt into the bargain.

'It is bad talk, N'gambi,' he said.

'And perhaps Mr. Betts will have worse when he wakes,' was the answer.

Brandon felt in his hip pocket for a flask and let a small amount of the raw spirit trickle down the unconscious man's throat. Betts choked and stirred, then opened his eyes and blinked in the strong light.

'Sorry, Rex,' he muttered thickly. 'Something ... sort of happened. The fire ...'

'Don't talk yet,' advised Brandon gently. 'Just take things easy for a while.' He turned his head. 'N'gambi, will you go and see if you can salvage anything from the camp? The trucks were well away from our tents. There must be a lot of stuff down there intact.'

N'gambi nodded and darted away. Brandon sat and stared at Betts, whose eyes were closed again. Presently, however, the zoologist opened them again and grinned rather feebly. 'Did you find him?' he muttered.

Brandon frowned. 'Oh, you mean the unknown marksman?' he answered. 'Not yet. We were following his trail when we saw the smoke.'

Betts smiled again. His voice was stronger when he spoke again. 'We'll get him before we're through,' he said.

Brandon nodded. 'You bet!' he said.

Betts blinked and moved his hand over his face in a weary gesture. Then: 'You probably thought I'd started the fire when you saw it first,' he murmured. 'I didn't, Rex.'

'Of course you didn't,' said Brandon quietly. 'Don't talk any more till N'gambi comes back. Then we'll get you fixed up in a tent and brew some tea or something.'

'If you can find it,' said Betts a little gloomily. 'I have an idea that fellow Tulani took everything with him. I suppose they've gone, haven't they?'

Brandon eyed him thoughtfully. 'They'll be back,' he said at length. 'There'll be trouble if they aren't!'

'I heard Tulani talking to a dozen others just before the truck caught fire,' muttered Betts slowly. 'He was urging them all to desert while they still had their skins intact. That man is a menace.'

'How did the fire start?'

'Probably an accident. The driver was working on the engine when it happened. I'd been keeping everyone busy, like you said — cleaning petrol filters and little jobs of that sort. The next thing I knew there was a dull kind of explosion and the truck was burning madly.'

'Anyone hurt?'

Betts shook his head. 'No. The driver escaped with a singeing and a bad scare. I yelled to the rest of the men to get the fire extinguishers and put the flames out. That was Tulani's chance. He just laughed at the notion. I tried to make a grab at the signal pistol in my belt with the idea of firing it into the air. Then someone else pushed me sideways, tripped me up and knocked me on the back of the head. That's all I can remember, until you came along.'

Brandon's lips tightened to a hard, thin line. 'I see,' he said quietly. 'Well, you did all you could.' He looked up at a sound behind him. 'Ah, N'gambi! What luck?'

'Better than I thought it would be,' came the reply. 'There is much food and other things in the tents. My worthless comrades left in too great a hurry to take everything with them. The fire is dying out now, which is also a good thing. We can return to the tents if Mr. Betts is strong enough.'

Betts heaved himself up on one elbow. 'I'll make it!' he said stoutly. 'Just you try me!'

Brandon grinned and helped him to his feet with care. Betts was dizzy and sick, swaying about as he clutched at Brandon. Then N'gambi took his other arm and together the three of them started back towards the smoke-hazed clearing.

Between them they got Betts down on one of the camp beds and made him comfortable. Apart from the crack on the head he was none the worse for his unpleasant experience, but it would be some days before he got rid of the headache that racked him every time he moved.

N'gambi quickly lit one of the stoves while Brandon made a compress for Betts' head. When that was done and the three of them were sipping tea inside Brandon's tent they discussed the position. Even Betts took part in the talk, and Brandon did not have the heart to keep him quiet.

It soon became clear that they would not

see the trucks again. The three of them were entirely dependent on their own resources. Brandon was faced with the problem of whether to carry on with his original plan, or turn back. The latter course of action went against his determination to finish a job once it was begun, but he could not plunge his companions into danger unless they were agreeable.

Aloud he said: 'How do you feel about it, N'gambi, are you ready to carry on with me? We shall have to walk, of course.'

N'gambi straightened his tall frame proudly.

'Where you go, I shall be honoured to follow.'

Brandon inclined his head. 'Thank you, N'gambi,' he murmured. 'I knew I could rely on you.' He turned and smiled at Betts where the little man lay on the camp-bed. 'What about it, Arthur?' he asked. 'Are you still keen to locate those gorillas of yours?'

Betts grinned boyishly. The large white bandage round his head moved as he nodded.

'You'd have a difficult job in keeping me back!' he said.

'That's what I thought,' replied Brandon with a smile.

It was agreed. N'gambi left the tent to collect provisions, but Betts lingered.

Brandon guessed what was coming. 'Before we fix this up, Rex,' said Betts, 'I should like to clear up a few points. Can we talk plainly?'

Brandon nodded.

'All right,' he said. 'You want to know what's going on, don't you?' He smiled as he spoke, putting Betts at his ease.

'You didn't trust me a while ago,' stated Betts. 'I knew that; but there wasn't much I could do about it. You're not on a hunting trip, are you?'

Brandon pursed his lips momentarily. Betts would have to know the details in the end; he might as well take him into his confidence at this stage rather than wait until later on. Deep inside him he knew he could trust Betts, despite the vague suspicions he had previously harboured.

'No,' he said slowly. 'We might as well understand each other, Betts. The hunting is a blind. You mentioned my being a geologist, and you also said that I wasn't the first geologist to penetrate these regions. A man called Georg Traski was here. Then Steven Shaw and his daughter. They were after a very rare mineral, but have never been heard of again.' He paused. 'I'm after the same mineral, Arthur. And I'm also after the man who tried to kill me last night.'

Betts nodded. 'I rather guessed there was something of that sort behind the trip,' he answered. 'I joined you in all innocence, and if you imagined I was an international spy I can only say I'm sorry. Can we work together?'

Brandon held out his hand in silence.

'Now I'm going after that man!' stated Brandon 'You'll have to remain here for a time, old chap, but N'gambi and I won't be longer than we can help. We shall leave everything you need close at hand, so take it easy. When we get back we'll pack up and start our little walk — deeper into the interior!'

Leaving Betts where he was, Brandon and N'gambi set out to trail the man whose footprints they had already started to follow earlier on.

As they left the site of the burnt-out

camp, the strains of 'Trees' reached their ears. Betts had been delighted when N'gambi reported that his gramophone was undamaged.

They exchanged grins as they plodded through the bush, side by side.

After several hours' painstaking tracking which carried them deep into the forest, over hills and through valleys of swampy ground and dense lush vegetation, Brandon called a halt.

'He can't have come much further than this,' he said.

'His tracks are fresh,' N'gambi asserted. 'What will you do when we catch up with him?'

'Depends,' answered Brandon laconically.

They ate a hasty meal from their haversacks, pressing on with little respite.

It was half an hour later that they saw the swamp. It lay before them in a hollow, thick and green and noisome, the faint wraiths of mist rising sluggishly from its surface.

But it was not so much the swamp itself, or even the miniature island of solid, mist-shrouded land that humped in the middle of it, which centred their attention. It was the grim scene on the shelving bank of the island. Brandon ran forward, cocking his high-velocity rifle as he moved. Then he stopped abruptly, raised the gun to his shoulder and aimed with the utmost care.

7

The Girl from the Mist

Swaying together in mortal combat were a white man and a leopard. The animal was one of the largest that Brandon had ever seen. Its claws were tearing at the man's chest, ripping the flesh from the bones as it struggled to get him down. The man, on his part, must have been attacked unexpectedly, for his rifle lay several yards away on the very edge of the swamp, where the bank of the island dropped away and disappeared in the evil-looking mud and slime that surrounded it.

As Brandon was taking aim at the leopard, the man broke free for an instant, only to stagger and fall full-length. The wild animal immediately launched itself in a mighty spring that carried it right onto him, pinning him down with its weight and its savage, tearing claws.

The vicious crack of Brandon's rifle cut

through the forest, momentarily drowning the snarls of the leopard and the stifled cries of the man.

Then the leopard reared upwards, tottered on its hind legs for a moment and fell sideways, beating at the air with its forelegs and thrashing wildly about in its death throes.

The torn and bleeding man rolled away, but only for a few feet before lying still.

'Come on, N'gambi!' snapped Brandon. 'We've got to cross that swamp somehow or other. He may not be dead!'

'*Bwana*, unless there is another man close by, we have found he who tried to kill you. The tracks lead straight to the edge of the swamp. If he is already dead it is good!'

But Brandon was taking no heed. He led the way down the slope into the fetid hollow, halting at the fringe of dark green slime that stretched for fifty yards to the solid ground of the little island. Straining his eyes through the haze of moisture that rose from the watery mud, he saw that the man had not stirred. The leopard, after a final twitch of its muscles, was also still.

'We must cross,' he said quietly.

N'gambi shook his head doubtfully, then seized a pole from the ground and prodded the swamp.

Brandon stepped gingerly into the mud. It rose to his knees as he started wading forward, feeling his way with care.

He and N'gambi had covered only a yard or two in this way when they stopped suddenly, gaping towards the island in mutual amazement.

From the thick undergrowth, made thicker by the mist that shrouded the island, a slight figure came into view, running towards the prone figure of the man on the shore.

'A girl, by all that's holy!' exclaimed Brandon. He raised his voice to a shout and hailed her. She waved her hand in reply, bent swiftly over the man on the ground, then straightened up abruptly, cupping her hands to her mouth.

'Stay where you are! You'll never get across unless you know the way. Stay there and wait for me!'

Brandon turned his head and glanced at N'gambi, who was watching the girl goggle-eyed as she started wading into the slime and mud.

Brandon's mind was whirling. Who was this girl? She was dressed in rags, her dark hair was loose and long and her skin was so deeply tanned as to be almost mahogany. He watched as she picked her way through the swamp by a twisting, tortuous route. Sometimes she was waist deep, moving gingerly with arms raised.

And then she was close to where Brandon and N'gambi were standing at the edge of the swamp. Brandon reached out and grasped her wrist, drawing her clear of the stinking mud and green-scummed water with a heave of his powerful shoulders.

'Oh, thank heaven you found me at last!' she gasped with a heartfelt sigh. 'I thought I should stay there for the rest of my life! It's been so awful.'

Brandon smiled as she sank to the ground and lowered her head, breathing fast.

'Take it gently,' he told her. 'You're all right now.'

She looked up, pushing the tangled hair from her forehead with one dirt-stained hand. The motion left a smear of mud on her brow. Brandon met her gaze. Her eyes were warm and brown behind the strain and near-starvation that marked her face. Then slowly she smiled at him.

'That man on the island,' said Brandon. 'Is he ...?'

She nodded quickly. 'Dead,' she answered briefly.

'Friend of yours?'

A tremor of fear crossed her face. 'No,' she whispered tensely. 'Take me away from this place. Please!'

Brandon realised she was suffering from shock and strain pretty badly. He looked across at N'gambi, jerking his head very slightly. Then he lifted the girl to her feet.

'Can you walk?' he inquired.

'Yes. Yes, of course I can. Just a bit shaken, that's all, Mr. ... What's your name?' She eyed him with sudden curiosity.

'Brandon,' he said. 'Rex Brandon. This is N'gambi. And you?'

Her eyes widened for an instant. 'I thought you knew!' she muttered. 'I'm Coralie Shaw.' There was a swift touch of bitterness in her voice as she said it.

'And the dead man yonder?'

'Nino Vasca. He — he was a swine! He's

kept me a prisoner and a slave for weeks and weeks. Ever since he came across me wandering, lost in the forest after Father was killed.'

Brandon didn't press her for fuller details. It was obviously a painful subject, but he knew that sooner or later the whole story would emerge. So Steven Shaw was dead, he thought grimly. Had he found what he set out to find before he died? He refrained from asking the girl.

'I'm afraid you'll have to wait until we get back to camp before cleaning up and changing. Let's go, shall we?'

She smiled again, hesitantly. 'Don't worry about it,' she told him. 'I've been living in a filthy little hut made of leaves and boughs for a long time. Any conditions would be heaven after that!' She shivered as she turned and followed N'gambi as he led the way through the tangled undergrowth and struck up the slope, retracing the path he and Brandon had already travelled. Brandon threw one last glance at the dead man and the dead leopard on the island in the swamp. Then he turned his back on the grim scene and followed in the footsteps of the girl and N'gambi.

For the most part they walked in silence, all their strength being required for the arduous journey through undergrowth and savage thorn scrub.

Brandon turned things over in his mind as he strode along. More than once his eyes came to rest on the slim back of the girl in front of him. Sometimes she turned her head and smiled at him. In spite of her past experiences she seemed to have a wonderful fund of strength on which to draw now that she was no longer a prisoner of the mysterious Nino Vasca, but a free woman among friends.

The sun was already dipping when they halted for a brief respite. It was during the stop that Brandon first hinted at the state of affairs Coralie could expect when they reached the camp.

'We were not out looking for you when we struck the swamp, Miss Shaw,' he said. 'I was fired on last night by a man with a rifle. N'gambi and I were tracking him down when we came on you. I'm assuming now that this Nino Vasca was the man who tried to kill me.'

She nodded slowly. 'Yes,' she said. 'He spoke about it when he returned. He'd been on a short hunting trip and it seems that he chanced on your camp. Then there was something to do with a lion after dark. Being a fugitive, he fired at you instinctively. He got back to the island early this morning. He seemed nervous; was under the impression that you and your party were probably searching for *him*!'

Brandon smiled grimly. 'I assure you we weren't,' he said, 'But who was he? You haven't told me that yet.'

She gestured with her hand. 'Of course!' she said. 'My mind isn't too clear, I'm afraid. There's been so much ... Vasca was an escaped convict from some settlement over in Portuguese territory. He was trekking East across the continent, I think. Then he found me and decided to lie low in the forest for a time. He kept me with him and finally located the swamp and the island. It seemed a good place to hide out in, and more by luck than anything else he discovered a way across the swamp itself. We've been there ever since.'

'Couldn't you have got away?'

She shook her head. 'It wasn't until yesterday that I felt sure enough of the path through the swamp to attempt it,' she said. 'I meant to go today in any event, but it wouldn't have been at all easy. I used to watch Vasca whenever he crossed the water, marking the twists of the path in my mind. Then the leopard got him and I knew my luck had changed.' She raised her eyes to Brandon's face, looking at him gravely. 'You were an unexpected factor, Mr. Brandon,' she added quietly.

Brandon grinned. 'I'm afraid I haven't a lot to offer you,' he said. 'Only sweat and toil, as they say. You see, something happened at my own camp. A series of accidents scared the men. The lion incident was the last straw. They deserted us, taking the trucks and stores. My only remaining companion was knocked on the head. He's back at camp now, recovering.'

'Oh …' she murmured. 'Then we ought to hurry on our way. As it is, it will be almost dark by the time we get there.'

'It's not much further now,' he told her.

'That's good,' she said with relief. 'Frankly, I'm getting tired.'

They set off again shortly afterwards. Brandon still did not mention his real purpose in being in the interior, thinking it better to wait until Coralie had grown accustomed to the circumstances. He knew that in all fairness to the girl he ought to start back for civilisation, but if he could persuade her to throw in her lot with himself and Betts, her knowledge would be invaluable. His greatest desire at the moment was to carry on his quest for the irikum deposits. Whether or not it would be possible depended to a great extent on how the girl herself felt about it. Nor did he press her for details as to the disaster which had obviously overtaken her father's expedition and stranded her in the wilds, at the mercy of a man like Nino Vasca.

That would come out later, he thought.

Another hour's trek brought them to the vicinity of the camp where Betts had been left. The air was still heavy with the reek of smouldering grass and burnt oil.

Coralie looked at Brandon inquiringly.

'The fuel truck caught fire,' he said briefly. 'That was just another of our misfortunes. What with that and the Borwingi drums to disturb our sleep we've been enjoying ourselves!'

Coralie shivered. 'How I've come to hate those drums!' she said. 'They've haunted me ever since Vasca found the swamp and the island. Sometimes they've been loud, sometimes soft, but always there, at night, in the background.'

'I can understand your feelings,' he remarked. 'And I doubt if we've heard the last of them, either.' He paused. 'Not that I think the Borwingi would show themselves hostile to us.'

She shot him a glance. 'It would depend on a lot of things,' she answered cryptically.

Brandon raised his eyebrows, but the girl made no further comment.

They topped a rise and glimpsed the blackened clearing of the camp site through the low growing baobab trees, which hereabouts were thick.

'Nearly home!' said Brandon, with a lightness he did not feel.

It was then that something about the camp struck him as being wrong, different to when he had seen it last. For an instant he was uncertain of the change, then it dawned on him with blinding force.

The tent in which Betts had been lying was flattened as if some heavy weight had thrust it over violently. On the ground were scattered odds and ends that Brandon recognised as having been inside when he last saw Betts.

N'gambi halted abruptly, turning startled eyes to Brandon.

'It is bad! *Bwana* Betts is no more!'

Brandon wasted no words in making an answer. He ran forward with the other two close behind him. With heart beating fast, he tore aside the flattened tent canvas, but it was quickly evident that Arthur Betts had gone.

The flimsy camp bed was overturned and blankets lay in heaps on the ground. Standing up and looking at N'gambi, Brandon said: 'What could have happened?'

The seasoned tracker shook his head in puzzlement.

'I cannot tell! But I will search. If he walked away, we shall find him. If something carried him off, we shall find a trail. You wait; I go see what I can.'

He turned and started casting round for

signs. In the meantime, Brandon carried out a more thorough search of the tent. Coralie, almost as worried as he was, helped him, though she barely knew what he was looking for. Nor did Brandon for that matter. He checked off a number of items he remembered having seen before. He did it automatically. And then it dawned on him that something was missing. It was perhaps the last thing he would have expected to be missing under the circumstances.

'What is it?' demanded the girl.

'Odd,' murmured Brandon. 'The gramophone's gone. We left Betts with it beside him.'

She shrugged helplessly. 'I don't understand any of this,' she admitted. 'Maybe N'gambi will discover something in the bush.'

They stood up straight and glanced round, looking for him, but N'gambi was nowhere to be seen. Brandon frowned and began to walk in the direction where he had last seen him.

He and Coralie were close to the fringe of the scrub when Brandon stopped in his tracks, eyes darting this way and that.

'We're not alone,' he said under his breath.

Coralie began to say something in answer, then the words froze on her lips.

From the undergrowth came movement. Brandon gripped his revolver tightly. The foliage parted before him, to reveal the menacing faces of war-painted warriors.

Others appeared on either side. In a moment Brandon and the frightened girl were confronted by more than a score of Borwingi tribesmen. Their bodies were streaked with ochre, and the sinking sun caught the blades of spears as they flashed.

Before Brandon or his companion could make a move they were surrounded.

8

Quana Strikes

Hemmed in on all sides by the circle of Borwingi warriors, Brandon and Coralie Shaw stood rigidly, peering round at the death that seemed ready to strike.

'Don't let 'em see we're afraid,' whispered Brandon.

She shivered. 'They must have got N'gambi already,' she answered nervously.

The blades of the warriors' spears came closer, stopping within inches of their flesh. Brandon counted the chances if he used his revolver. He could probably hit two or three if it came to it, but he knew that as soon as he fired it would be all up with himself and the girl.

Then one of the warriors raised his spear high and thrust his head forward towards Brandon. Speaking in Borwingi tongue, he said:

'You are our prisoners, white man! It is

93

well that you walk with us quietly. Throw down your fire stick!'

Brandon hesitated for only a second. He had left his rifle across by the tent. N'gambi had been carrying another rifle when he disappeared. Instead of dropping his revolver immediately, he said: 'If we come with you quietly you must take us to your chief.'

The Borwingi stared at him unsmilingly. 'It shall be done, white man. Borwingi warriors keep their word — even to their enemies.'

Brandon dropped his revolver on to the ground at his feet.

'Come!' said the warrior, jerking his head towards the bush.

'Lucky I know their lingo,' muttered Brandon. 'I've met Borwingis before, but they didn't act like this. Can't make it out. Something must be wrong.'

Coralie drew a deep breath as she started forward with Brandon. Borwingis pressed them closely on all sides, their spears never far away.

Some distance from the camp the party was joined by another, smaller group.

'They've got N'gambi,' said the girl excitedly. 'Oh, I'm so glad they didn't kill him!'

Brandon said nothing. He was puzzled by their capture, and in spite of the fact that no harm had so far come to them, he did not give a lot for their chances considering the present mood.

With no word spoken, the reinforced party penetrated deeper into the thickly growing bush of thorn and acacia. Brandon decided that Arthur Betts must have been captured earlier, which would account for his disappearance. He was more worried about the future than he cared to admit.

Moving easily through the maze of jungle-like forest, their captors at last brought them to a small clearing which formed a village. Mud huts were clustered in the middle of the clearing. They were centred around one hut much larger than the rest.

Seated on a kind of veranda in front of it was an imperious-looking man, decked out in tribal finery that proclaimed him to be a man of immense importance.

'The chief,' whispered Brandon to Coralie.

They were halted none too gently in front of the veranda on which the chief was seated. He raised his right arm and peered at them intently. His face was expressionless.

Brandon waited for the Borwingi chief to make the first move. He contented himself with lifting an arm in salute. The action was carried out with considerably more bravado than he actually felt, for he realised only too well that he and the girl, as well as N'gambi, were in a tight spot.

The chief acknowledged the bows of his warriors, then rose to his feet and stood looking down at the captives with cold, grave eyes that gave nothing away.

One of the warriors spoke to him, telling him that the white man could speak their language. The chief gave a curt nod.

'Then you will not die without knowing the reason,' he said to Brandon. 'It is well. We are a people who embrace justice whenever we can, but after losing so many of our women, children and old men we can show no mercy to the white invaders of the forest. You, the woman with you, and your servant will die by the sacrificial spear when the sun is gone to rest. I, Sempandi, Great

Chief of the Borwingi tribes, have spoken.'

Brandon listened to this condemnation with an open mouth. He could not understand it, but intended to find out what the chief was talking about.

'Great Chief,' he said firmly, 'you speak in riddles. How is it that you connect us with the loss of your men, women and children? We have done them no harm, nor even seen your people until they took us prisoner.'

The chief stared at him narrowly. Then: 'Your coming has roused the mighty Quana to anger,' he said. 'It is since you entered our country that Quana has come in the night and carried off many of our people. Quana strikes. He is angry because of you! When you are dead, he will no longer trouble us.'

Brandon frowned, glancing sideways at Coralie.

'Who is Quana, Great Chief?' he inquired. 'We are ignorant of his name.'

'Quana is the mighty gorilla which dwells in the forest a day's march from here,' came the answer. The chief's voice was grave when he spoke. 'Quana must be pacified.

He has already carried off one of your white companions. He will be pleased when we kill the woman and yourself.'

Brandon looked at Coralie. 'So Betts was carried off by a gorilla!' he muttered. 'Funny, but he came all this way to look for one! Poor old Arthur, it looks as if he got rather more than he wanted.'

Brandon met the chief's gaze again, steadily and without fear.

'Great Chief,' he began in a loud, clear voice, 'I offer sympathy for the loss of your tribesmen, but have a suggestion to make which will save further trouble and bloodshed.'

'Do not expect to save your lives by false words.'

'I speak no false words, Sempandi. I speak as a mighty hunter of wild creatures, as a warrior like yourself.'

Chief Sempandi hesitated, impressed by Brandon's tone.

'Speak, white man!' he said at length. 'We, the great Borwingi, will listen to your words. That is all we promise.'

'It is just,' answered Brandon, nodding gravely. 'Why do you not rid yourselves of the threat?'

Sempandi blinked a little. Then: 'We have already tried,' he replied. 'Quana is a cunning creature. His wiles are greater than the wisdom of our warriors. Quana will go on living in the forest though we send out a hundred spears against him.'

Brandon smiled slightly. 'I have weapons that can kill at a greater distance than spears,' he answered simply. 'If you are willing, and you guide me to the haunts of Quana, I will undertake to kill him in return for the safety of my companions and myself. Is it agreed, Great Sempandi?'

Brandon waited with fast-beating heart, not knowing how his suggestion would be received. The chief peered at him intently for a moment. Then: 'These words must be considered by the council,' he said. 'Our warriors have been close to Quana; but always he slips away out of range of their spears. They have set traps for him; but his cunning is so great that none have worked.'

'Think it over,' said Brandon. He had a hunch that he might have saved their lives, but a lot would depend on whether he could find and kill the gorilla that menaced the Borwingi village. It was strange, he reflected, that a gorilla had turned savage in this way. Usually they were peaceable creatures, living their own lives and not interfering with other things. This Quana must have turned a sort of rogue, he thought grimly. In which case it would be far more dangerous than many other wild animals he had faced.

'Take the prisoners away and keep them safe!' ordered Sempandi.

Brandon and the girl were hustled to one of the nearest huts and thrust inside through the small half-round opening that served as a door. N'gambi was taken to another hut. They looked at each other in the semi-gloom, then Brandon grinned reassuringly.

'Keep your chin up, Coralie,' he murmured. 'We aren't dead yet by a long chalk.'

'Hard to believe,' she answered with a rueful smile.

Two warriors stood guard outside the entrance of the hut, their spears glinting in the rays of the setting sun. It would be useless to attempt an escape, even if

Brandon had been willing to try it.

They talked quietly together, he and the girl. Time dragged endlessly, 'til the sun was almost swallowed below the line of tree tops.

'It's getting late,' said Coralie nervously. 'I wish we knew what they've decided.'

Brandon started to answer, then a shadow fell across the entrance of the hut. The figure of a tall Borwingi stooped and entered. Brandon watched him narrowly. The warrior stared at him hard for a moment, then nodded, turning to someone else outside.

'It is he, the great hunter,' he said. 'He saved my life many moons back when death threatened me in a great river flood. This white man is my friend. He is the friend of all men, save those who are evil. If he says he will rid us of Quana, he will do it.'

Brandon glanced at Coralie. Then he smiled. 'Good heavens!' he muttered. 'Just imagine that!'

Coralie grinned admiringly. 'Lucky for us you make a habit of saving people's lives,' she whispered.

A moment later, Chief Sempandi entered

the hut. Brandon rose to meet him gravely.

'It is well, white man *bwana*,' said the chief. 'I am sorry if our treatment of yourself and your woman has not been hospitable. We did not know who you were and you did not tell us.'

'I feel no ill-will, Sempandi,' answered Brandon quietly. 'May we not renew the friendship that exists between us?'

'It is understood,' replied the chief. 'A feast has already been ordered. In the morning you shall hunt and kill Quana! Any man who saves the life of one of our people is a friend. I, Sempandi, have spoken!'

Brandon hid his utter relief. His fingers closed over Coralie's wrist in an instinctive gesture of joy. Then they were leaving the hut and walking in company with the chief towards the big dwelling that served as his palace. They were all to remember that evening in the Borwingi village for the rest of their lives. Nothing but kindness was shown them, yet Brandon was on edge all the time, thinking of Arthur Betts and the fate that must have overtaken him. It cast a shadow over his enjoyment, and he was thankful when at last the singing and dancing and feasting were over and the chief took him aside for discussion about the coming hunt.

It was arranged that a small party of half a dozen tribal hunters and trackers should accompany Brandon. Two men had already been dispatched to Brandon's old camp to retrieve his rifles. N'gambi, who had, of course, been released to join his companions, would go with them. The only thing that worried Brandon a little was the fact that Coralie insisted on going after Quana with them. But under the circumstances, he could not really blame her.

Dawn found them ready to leave. They were given a ceremonial send-off according to the rites of the Borwingi tribe.

Brandon soon learnt that Quana dwelt in the forest beyond the swamp where he had first met Coralie Shaw. The tribal hunters made considerably faster time than he himself had done with N'gambi on the previous day. They had paths through the undergrowth which they knew well. Progress was so good that before noon the chief guide informed Brandon that very soon now they would be close to the tree in which Quana lived.

Brandon nodded and called a halt. Then he picked N'gambi and one of the Borwingis, going ahead and leaving the rest of the party behind. Coralie would have liked to have gone with him, but he was firm. If an enraged gorilla ran amok it was a dangerous adversary, and with Quana there was no knowing what to expect.

N'gambi handed him the most powerful rifle he possessed, a .55 elephant gun. Brandon took it and checked the magazine. Then he jerked his head to the Borwingi and his bearer.

'Come!' he said softly. 'It is now that the moment of triumph is near. *Bwana* Betts will be avenged!'

N'gambi nodded in reply, speaking to the Borwingi with enthusiasm. Brandon motioned for silence as they advanced through the bush and scrub that barred their way.

The Borwingi said: '*Bwana*, it is close now. Quana has ears all round him. Make no noise.'

They crept forward. Even Brandon was

a little breathless and tense as his footsteps crunched softly on the crisp vegetation underfoot. He gripped his rifle and keyed himself up for instant action.

N'gambi glanced sideways at Brandon, who he now looked on with renewed respect after their miraculous escape from death at the hands of the Borwingi.

The Borwingi guide advanced stealthily, halting every now and again to listen and sniff at the air. The sun was well up in the heavens by this time. Torpid heat welled from the earth around them. Brandon felt the sweat running down his back in rivulets, damping the bush-shirt he wore. Then the Borwingi stopped abruptly, head on one side.

Brandon looked at the ground, at broken branches on the thorn bushes around him. Quana had passed this way. He felt an urgency inside him to press on; but something stopped him from speaking to the Borwingi guide. The man's odd expression caught his attention. Suddenly the man turned and stared at him fearfully.

'Hark, *bwana*!' he whispered. 'There is music of a strange kind in the air. The mighty Quana must be very angry with our people to make such a noise.'

Brandon listened intently. The faint music of 'Trees' reached his sensitive ears.

9

The Valley of Devils

'Betts' gramophone!' he whispered incredulously. 'Well, at any rate it gives us a line.' He was speaking half to himself. The Borwingi did not understand his words, but N'gambi nodded briefly.

'Come,' he murmured softly.

They started forward again, more swiftly now that they had a definite indication as to where Quana might be. The sound of the gramophone came from fifty or sixty yards away. As they advanced, Brandon decided that no gorilla in the world would have the comprehension or intelligence to work a gramophone. A great hope filled him as he thrust a way through the undergrowth that cut off their view of Quana's tree-top dwelling.

Then the Borwingi guide halted and lifted his right arm to point. He was staring ahead with widened eyes.

Brandon stopped dead, looking up and forwards at the strangest sight he had ever witnessed. Twenty feet from the ground, in the fork of a tall tree, was a rough platform of boughs. Standing at one end of the platform, long hairy arms almost touching the boughs that formed it, was the biggest gorilla Brandon had seen in all his big game hunting experience. It was also the first gorilla he had seen that was under the spell of music, for such was the case. The massive creature was swaying to and fro with monotonous regularity, keeping ponderous time to the rhythm of the tune.

And sitting hunched up as far away from the animal as he could get was Arthur Betts, pale and exhausted as he kept his gramophone going continuously.

It was then that N'gambi, careless for an instant, put his foot on a dry twig. The sudden crack changed the scene before them with alarming speed.

Quana stopped his swaying abruptly, lumbering round to peer toward the little group on the ground some distance away. Arthur Betts saw Brandon at the same time. Instinctively he uttered a shout of mingled joy and relief. It was too much for Quana. With an unexpectedly swift lurch the great ape whirled about and hurled himself at Betts.

Brandon brought the heavy elephant rifle up to his shoulder as quickly as lightning. In a split second he drew a bead on Quana, squeezing the trigger calmly and with care, although he knew that the life of Betts depended on the shot.

The crashing report echoed through the forest, mingling with Betts' startled cry and the bellowing roar of Quana.

Quana's mighty fists closed convulsively, not on Betts, but on the small black case of the gramophone. The impact of Brandon's steel-coated bullet smashed into the gorilla as it grabbed the instrument.

Then Brandon was running forward with N'gambi and the Borwingi guide close at his heels. They had almost reached the base of the tree when the twitching body of Quana toppled downwards, dark blood oozing from a jagged hole at the nape of his neck.

The thud of the falling body literally shook the ground.

Brandon approached the inert monster cautiously, not sure if it was lifeless. But he need not have worried. The mighty Quana would no longer terrorise the forest or the tribe of Borwingi.

Hanging from the platform dwelling of the monster was a plaited rope of lianas. Brandon looked upwards to see the figure of Betts climbing slowly down. He and N'gambi steadied the crude rope until Betts was a few feet from the ground, then they grabbed him firmly as he fell into their arms, exhausted from his terrifying ordeal.

Hardly had they got him on his feet again when the rest of the hunting party, including Coralie, broke into view and joined them. The Borwingis were jubilant, dancing round the carcase of Quana and thrusting at it with their spears.

Betts, still badly shaken, told Brandon he had been winding the gramophone for hours on end. His greatest fear had been that the spring of the instrument would break, for he was convinced that he owed his life to the music of 'Trees'.

Now the gramophone was smashed, for Quana had carried it down to the ground with him when he fell mortally wounded.

Brandon sympathised with Betts at the loss of his precious music, but secretly decided that after all this time he could well do without it himself.

Despite his ordeal, Betts was in good shape, refusing any assistance on the way back to the Borwingi village. Several of the guides and hunters ran on ahead, carrying the good news to their chief. Others remained with the dead body of Quana, determined to guard it against carrion birds or jackals. It was proposed to take the body back to the village for skinning and a ceremonial burning of the carcase. Brandon would be presented with the skin as a trophy.

Back at the village they were feted once again, but all the time Brandon was thinking of carrying on with his search for Traski's irikum deposits. At a suitable moment when they were alone together, he broached the subject to Coralie. It was the first intimation the girl had had of Brandon's real mission to the interior.

'Look, Coralie,' he began slowly, 'I don't want to ask you anything you'd rather not answer, but you may have guessed already that I'm not on a hunting safari pure and simple.'

The girl met his gaze with level eyes. The two of them were standing in the semi-gloom of a thatched mud hut.

'I've had ideas,' she admitted. 'You're well known as a geologist, aren't you? Although I haven't said anything about it, I've had a hunch that you might be following in my father's footsteps. It was lucky for me that you were.'

Brandon nodded. 'You're making it easy for me,' he said with a smile. 'Your father was seeking irikum, wasn't he? Georg Traski found it, but was lost himself. Then your father's expedition vanished. Yes, I'm after the same thing.' He turned away and stared out through the half-round entrance of the little hut. 'The international situation in Europe and the rest of the world has made it more imperative than ever that I find the stuff.'

The girl came close up behind him. 'You want me to help you, don't you?' she said very quietly. 'You needn't have asked, Rex. My father and I failed because we ran

112

into trouble; but I know that if he could have carried on to the Valley of Devils he'd have done what he set out to do. If you're determined to take up where he left off you can count on me.' Her eyes were grave and sober as she talked. Brandon, who had turned when she began, put his hands on her shoulders.

'Good woman!' he said. 'I had a feeling you'd react like that.' He broke off. Then: 'What happened to your party, Coralie?'

She hesitated for a moment. 'More or less what happened to your own, I suppose,' she said at length. 'We heard drums and the men got scared. They were going to desert us. I'm sure they'd have done it if fate hadn't stepped in and taken the decision out of their hands.'

'How did it happen?' he inquired.

'Nothing to do with the Borwingi tribe or anything like that,' she continued. 'We were crossing a river infested with crocs. It was the rainy season and the place was in flood. The rafts we used overturned and most of the men were drowned. We lost all the stores except one light truck that my father and I were using. Fortunately for us, we'd already crossed and were waiting for the main party.

'The few bearers left alive after the disaster took to their heels and disappeared, leaving us entirely alone in the jungle. We carried on for a time because Father thought he could at least find out if his information was correct before turning back. Then ...' She broke off, gesturing with her hand in a helpless manner.

'Your father was killed, is that it?' he put in gently.

She nodded. 'Yes,' she said quietly. 'The truck was bogged in a swamp we ran into unexpectedly. We tried to get it out and failed. It was while we were doing that that a lion showed up and caught us unawares. It sprang at Dad before I could reach a gun. When I killed the lion, Dad was already dead.'

'And you started to trek back home then ... I'm sorry about it, Coralie. You've had a pretty rough deal one way and another. It seems hardly fair to ask you to carry on after what you've told me.'

'Now that I know what you're after I'm perfectly ready to,' she insisted. 'If Father was still alive he'd want me to, I know. Besides, I think I have information as to the location of these irikum deposits.'

'The Valley of Devils … That's a name I haven't heard before,' he mused. 'How did your father come to connect it with Traski?'

She shrugged. 'My father was as close a friend of Traski as any man ever could be,' she explained. 'I never met him myself, but Father seemed positive he was on the right track. He mentioned that Traski had let a few things drop when they'd been talking together.'

'I see,' murmured Brandon thoughtfully. 'In that case your help will be invaluable. For my own part, I was relying more or less on instinct and the fact that N'gambi had been a guide to Traski for part of his first safari. Now it looks as if we've got some more definite clues to go on.'

She nodded eagerly. 'The only snag is that Father never gave me exact instructions on how to find the Valley of Devils,' she said.

Brandon grinned. 'We'll find it!' he answered. 'If Chief Sempandi is approached in the right way, the odds are he'll lend us guides. I'm curious to know what sort of disaster wiped out Traski's party.'

The girl shrugged. 'In this country,' she said, 'anything could have happened.'

Shortly afterwards, Brandon, after consultation with Betts, had an interview with the chief. It was, however, a very disappointing one from Brandon's point of view.

'Take heed, white man,' said Sempandi grimly. 'Do not enter the Valley of Devils if you value your life or those of your friends. It is an evil place, harbouring only death for those who seek to penetrate it.'

'You know the place, Great Chief?' queried Brandon.

Sempandi inclined his massive head gravely. 'Never have I entered it or approached it, white man,' he answered; 'but others of your colour have done so, never to return. None of my people will go near it.'

'I am not afraid, nor are my friends,' replied Brandon. 'We intend to explore this valley, and would ask you to lend us your bravest warriors for guides. We do not ask them to enter the Valley of Devils, but to take us near it. Will you do this thing for me, Sempandi?'

But Sempandi only shook his head. 'You are a brave man, *bwana*, but foolish with it. I would not ask my warriors or hunters to face the danger that is unknown. All I can do is to give you directions for reaching the Valley of Devils if you still desire to go there. But I have warned you it is unwise.'

Brandon had to be content with that. There was no way of shaking the chief's determination to protect his men.

After a few days' rest in the village, during which time they brought up all the stores and equipment they would need from the site of the burnt-out camp, the little party of four were ready to leave. Betts had by now fully recovered from his recent experiences; and the girl was eager to pick up the trail where her father had left it; only N'gambi was somewhat nervous about the future.

At the last moment before their departure, Chief Sempandi came to Brandon and with grave ceremony presented him and his companions with charms and powerful *ju-ju* against the unknown evils of the Valley of Devils.

'Many days' journey lie before you,

bwana,' he said. 'It is well that you take great care, for there is danger ahead.'

Brandon thanked him. A party of Borwingi warriors accompanied them for several miles, but nothing would persuade them to go any further. So the little group of adventurers made their way slowly and laboriously through the dense forest region that lay between themselves and the Valley of Devils.

There were moments of extreme excitement during the trek. Swamps and thickets of thorn barred their path and had to be overcome. Insects in hordes made life almost unbearable at times. Wild animals disturbed in their jungle haunts resented the party's intrusion. Since they had no transport each member of the group had to carry a load of supplies and equipment, though these had been reduced to the bare minimum before they had started.

On one occasion, three days before they reached the vicinity of the dreaded Valley of Devils, Brandon had the luck to save Coralie's life. It was an incident he was to remember in after years with a surge of thankfulness, for by this time the girl had grown to be a very close friend as well as companion on the mission in which he was engaged.

The incident occurred a moment or two after Brandon, who was in the lead, hacked his way through a particularly dense belt of liana-tangled scrub and thorn. Beyond the scrub was a small clearing, with more widely spaced trees on the far side. Brandon, carving a path with his machete, stood aside to let Coralie pass him into the open. Betts was close behind her, while N'gambi brought up the rear.

Then, just as Brandon turned his head, there was a violent crashing noise from the other side of the clearing. The girl stared past him with a look of dawning horror on her face. Brandon whirled round, dropping his machete as he did so and seizing a rifle from Betts, who was nearest.

Charging across the clearing, straight for Coralie, was an enormous, pale-grey rhinoceros, head down and wicked-looking horn thrust forward.

Brandon had to aim and fire more quickly than he could ever remember doing before. The rhinoceros was less than fifteen yards away, thundering down on them. For a moment it looked as if his shot would be too late, then the crashing concussion of the heavy-bore rifle drowned the squealing grunts of the tank-like creature. Coralie threw herself sideways, dragging Betts with her. N'gambi hurled his body into the thorn thicket. Brandon stood firm as the animal was carried forward by the impetus of its charge.

Standing calmly, he pumped another shot into it when it was less than five yards away, then side-stepped nimbly as it hurtled past, dead on its feet, to collapse in a twitching heap on the very spot where Coralie had been but an instant before.

Brandon whistled soundlessly. Then the others were running up, congratulating him on the incredible speed with which he had dealt with the emergency.

'It wouldn't have been so funny if I'd missed!' he said, his eyes on the girl. She was a little pale from the frightening experience, but thanked him with a smile.

No one mentioned it again, but Brandon and Coralie were both fully aware that without Brandon's lightning action she must inevitably have been caught by the rush of the rhinoceros.

Pressing on with as much speed as they could, they finally arrived in the lee of a forest-covered range of hills. A wide swamp separated the rising ground from the lower country; but after considerable trouble they eventually crossed it and stood on higher ground.

'Now then,' said Brandon, 'according to Sempandi, the Valley of Devils begins with a very narrow entrance that is marked by a single ancient monolith of stone. He told us it was two hours' march from the edge of the swamp at a place about a mile from where we crossed.'

'You're sure?' Betts sounded doubtful.

Brandon nodded firmly. 'Judging by the landmarks he gave us, yes,' he replied. 'Come on. With any luck we ought to reach the mouth of the valley in time to take a look before dusk.'

N'gambi threw a frightened look all round before lifting his load to his head again after the pause. Then they were moving once more, picking their way with the utmost care through a tangle of treacherous thorn and interwoven liana growth.

They came on the ancient monolith suddenly. What lost race had originally put it up they could only guess, but it certainly served as a landmark in their present quest. Cut in the rising ground that lay east of the swamp was a dark and uninviting path through the forest. It looked as if at some time in past aeons an earthquake had riven the hills and formed this split in the ground. Now it was thickly choked with scrub and low-growing baobab trees.

Brandon glanced at his companions. 'Shall we go in now or wait 'til morning?' he asked.

'Just a little way in,' suggested Coralie quickly. 'I'm so anxious to take a look I can't wait another night!'

Brandon grinned. 'All right,' he said, looking up at the sky. 'We must be outside again in an hour though. I don't think it would be wise to remain in the valley all night until we know more about it.'

They started in cautiously, conscious of utter silence. No birds sang, no monkeys chattered. Even the insects were less insistent. For the first time they sensed the eeriness of the place.

Then Coralie suddenly stopped, a cry choked back on her lips. Brandon whirled round, to see her pointing aghast at a spot just off the narrow path. Her eyes were filled with horror.

10

Devils or Men?

'My God!' breathed Betts in an awed whisper. 'What on earth could have happened to them?'

N'gambi's eyes were wide with fear as he gazed at the things Coralie had seen in the thicket edging the path.

'Five of them,' said Brandon grimly. 'Five headless skeletons. What killed 'em, I wonder ...?'

'Devils!' answered N'gambi hoarsely. His teeth were beginning to chatter in the fading light. Hemmed in by steep sides, the forest-choked gorge in which they stood was already in semi-gloom. Brandon had misjudged the time by an appreciable margin. But so curious was he as to the fate that had overtaken those five men whose skeletons lay before him that he barely heeded the rapidly deepening gloom.

'Are they some of Georg Traski's safari

party?' asked Coralie quietly.

Brandon was kneeling on the soggy ground now, examining the skeletons. There was no trace of their skulls, but a few bits and pieces of what had once been leather equipment were readily discernible. White ants had cleaned the bones; but white ants had never removed the heads of the dead men.

Brandon straightened up and turned to Betts and the girl.

'Something of a mystery,' he observed. 'By the look of it, I should say this valley's inhabitants don't approve of visitors!' His voice was hard and grim.

The others glanced over their shoulders at his words.

Darkness was coming down on the Valley of Devils with alarming rapidity now. Clouds overhead thickened in the sky.

Betts began to speak, then the words died in his throat. Instinctive fear gripped the hearts of all of them. The air was suddenly full of a weird moaning sound. It began in a whisper from further up the narrow valley, then swelled and swelled into a near howl, gradually becoming steady after several seconds. Then it altered again, rising and falling in the most eerie cadence Brandon had ever heard. He felt the hair rising on the nape of his neck as he stared around for some sign of the origin of the noise, yet he knew it was not made by any human agency. The very realisation made him grasp his rifle more firmly. Betts was drawing his revolver and glancing this way and that, though there was no target in sight. Even Coralie was looking about, a rifle grasped in her capable hands.

Betts licked his lips nervously. 'What do you make of it, Rex?' he asked.

For answer, Brandon turned. 'I think we'd be wise to get out of here before the night comes down completely,' he said. 'It may be a natural phenomenon, but it certainly isn't good for the nerves. Come on, everybody!'

They had found the skeletons two or three hundred yards inside the narrow valley. Thick gloom was closing in around them as Brandon began to lead the way hurriedly towards the open.

But he had not gone far before he halted abruptly, rifle thrust forward at the ready, eyes keenly narrowed as they came to rest on the ghost of movement ahead which had caught his attention.

'What's up?' demanded Betts in an anxious whisper.

Brandon said nothing. An instant later the *swoosh* of an arrow reached their ears as the feather-flighted shaft twanged past close to Brandon's head. There was a thud as the arrow embedded itself in a tree somewhere on the other side of the pathway.

'Down!' yelled Brandon. He fired as he dropped, aiming in the general direction from which the arrow had come. Behind him came the sharp crack of Coralie's rifle, then the loud bang of N'gambi peppering the scrub with a shotgun. Betts could see nothing to shoot at, and before he loosed off his first round several more arrows had flicked over their heads and been lost in the darkness. What worried Brandon was the fact that they were apparently being shot at from front and rear. An arrow struck his pith helmet, narrowly missing his skull. He cursed and fired again, bringing forth a yell of agony from somewhere in the darkness.

Suddenly N'gambi set up a howl of

terror. Brandon glanced over his shoulder to see what had happened. His eyes widened as he glimpsed half a dozen luminous figures a few yards distant.

'Devils!' said N'gambi. 'They are devils!'

'Devils, my foot!' snapped Brandon tersely. 'They're painted men.' As he spoke he fired, bringing down one of the glowing figures which had had such a terrifying effect when they first appeared.

The four adventurers were lying in a group at the edge of the path now. Their guns spat death at the half-seen enemy. So far, none of their attackers had approached very close, but it was plain to Brandon and his friends that it would not be long before they did. It seemed inevitable that things would be bad for them when that happened.

'I can count about twenty of them,' said Coralie quietly. She fired again, tight-mouthed and determined to sell her life as dearly as she could. 'That's nineteen!' she muttered.

Brandon grunted. He ducked as an arrow whistled over, then snapped a shot at a luminous-painted form that suddenly darted into the line of his sights. The figure screamed, threw up its arms, and flopped in a lifeless huddle on the ground.

N'gambi brought cries of pain from two more as he emptied both barrels of the shotgun at a small group thirty yards up the path.

But in spite of their success, the party was hard pressed. Betts had received a superficial flesh wound from one of the arrows, while a spear had landed quivering in the earth so close to Brandon as to remind him that they had only escaped with their lives by the greatest luck — or because of the powerful *ju-ju* charms presented to them by Chief Sempandi.

'They're getting bolder now,' whispered Coralie. She wriggled herself a little closer to Brandon, edging in under the partial shelter and cover of a thorn bush.

'Keep your chin up,' Brandon replied. 'We'll make out all right.' He did not feel half as confident as he tried to sound, for it was pretty clear now that they would shortly be overwhelmed. Attacked from all sides, the four of them could not hold out indefinitely, especially in the darkness, which was now complete.

The painted figures of the enemy closed in around them. As fast as Brandon and his companions shot them down, more appeared from the thickets and close-growing scrub. Had they not been visible as ghostly forms streaked with white, it would have been impossible to hold out so long. But Brandon realised with a sickening sense of dismay that the end must come.

Between them they killed or wounded several more of the tireless natives. Recalling the five decapitated bodies, Brandon guessed that such would be their own fate if they were overwhelmed.

What would have happened, though, none of them ever knew, for just as their situation appeared to become impossible, there was a dramatic interruption.

Brandon was working the bolt of his rifle frantically. His eyes were narrowed as he stared at their attackers. Then to his amazement they melted from sight, slipping back into hiding.

'They're working up for something else!' breathed Coralie.

'I don't like this, Rex,' muttered Betts.

'What's the idea?'

'Can't tell!' snapped Brandon. 'I suggest we make a break for the entrance of the valley while we've got the chance. Run like the devil! Now!'

He was up on his feet, darting forward, one hand grasping Coralie's wrist. Betts and N'gambi brought up the rear.

But hardly had Brandon covered more than twenty yards when he was brought up short by a tall figure barring his way.

Had it not been for the fact that the man in front of him gripped a heavy Mauser automatic that was pointed straight at his chest, he might have tried to use his rifle — but as it was, Brandon decided that discretion would be better than bravado.

'Do not make another step!' snapped the man in the path. 'If you do you will die instantly. You are surrounded by my warriors, and I can kill you myself without danger!'

Brandon made no comment. He was staring at the weird-looking man with a puzzled frown on his forehead. There was something so grotesque about the bearded figure that he was robbed of speech. The figure was long-haired, wearing no hat. It was obvious that he was a white man; that much was plain even in the darkness. But a stranger white man Brandon had never seen. The figure wore a long white robe of some flowing material that was draped from his shoulders. Round his waist was a broad leather belt, from which hung the holster in which a second automatic pistol rested.

'You are wise!' said the man curtly when the whole party stopped in their tracks. His voice was strongly accented, so that though he was speaking in English it was a little hard to understand his words.

'No man is wise to court death,' answered Brandon slowly. 'Who are you and why do you treat us in this hostile manner?'

The man's eyes blazed with a queer, fanatical light. It was fairly clear to Brandon that they were face to face with a lunatic.

'You are in forbidden territory,' he snarled. 'Now you are my prisoners. No man enters the Valley of Devils and leaves it alive.'

'Who are you?' demanded Brandon boldly.

The man drew himself up to his full

height. His automatic never wavered as he covered the group.

'I am Georg Traski the First, King of the Valley of Devils!' came the proud announcement.

'*Traski?*' gasped Coralie breathlessly. 'But ... I don't understand!'

'Nor do I,' grunted Brandon. He glanced round, sizing up the chances of escape. They seemed pretty thin at the moment.

Traski uttered a strange cry. Even before the sound had faded there was movement in the undergrowth all round them. Forty or fifty of the luminous-painted warriors surged forward, completely surrounding the four invaders of the valley. If there had been the ghost of a chance of escape before, it was gone now. Brandon and his companions could only hope for the best. They were seized and disarmed before they fully realised what was happening. With incredible speed, they were tied hand and foot, lifted from the ground and slung from long poles, to be carried deeper into the Valley of Devils, like the spoils of a hunting trip.

In a state of bewildered apprehension

the four of them were carried further and further into the deep-sided, dark little valley. It was a place that seemed to breed fear with every yard of its length. Nothing stirred but the steady tramp of the unspeaking natives who carried them. Brandon had lost sight of Georg Traski, but his mind dwelt on the madman. By what means had Traski deposed the Chief of this tribe? By what power did Traski hold their allegiance?

He doubted if the man would show them much mercy unless they could win him over in some way. How they were to do a thing like that under the circumstances was entirely beyond Brandon. However, he was a man who always preferred to face major crises as and when they arose, and thrust aside the thought of dying with a firm determination.

None of the party spoke. The silent trek continued for more than an hour. At times the path was so narrow and twisting that even the native men were slowed in their advance.

But finally Brandon saw in the darkness that the valley was widening out into a bowl-shaped clearing, almost devoid of scrub and thorn. The faint light of stars from a now cloudless sky seeped down from above and lit the scene coldly. It was not until then that he had any real conception of the size of this tribe. Now he saw them strung out in file, nearly a hundred-strong. And far in front he glimpsed the tall, stoop-shouldered figure of Georg Traski, King of the Valley.

The long line of glowing warriors, uncanny in their streaks of luminous war-paint, wound slowly across the space, headed by Traski. Brandon saw the dark entrance of a cave on the far side of the bowl. Suddenly, the flickering light of a flaming torch sprang up inside it, shedding yellow glimmers of light on hard, rocky walls.

At the entrance of the cave they halted. The prisoners were dumped unceremoniously on the ground and their legs were freed. Jabbed upright with spear tips, they were herded into the gloomy cavern, which was of considerable size. They saw that Traski had enthroned himself on a skin-covered seat. All round were rich animal hides. They hung from the walls and carpeted the rocky floor of the cave.

Traski glared at them as more torches were lit. The natives lined the walls of the cave, leaving Brandon, Coralie, Betts and the terrified N'gambi standing a yard or two from Traski's throne.

Traski rose to his full height. Brandon stared back at the man defiantly.

'You have entered forbidden territory!' stated Traski in harsh tones. 'I have said it before, and I repeat it again to impress on you the crime you have committed. Only death can come of entering this valley! It is mine, and no one leaves once they enter. You are now condemned to die in a manner befitting your sins!'

Before Brandon could reply, Traski clapped his hands loudly. A number of the tribesmen ran forward, grasping the four hapless captives and dragging them further into the recesses of the cavern. More torches were lit and they saw that beyond the main cavern was another one, a little smaller, but higher in pitch.

'Water!' gasped Coralie. 'It's an underground lake or something.'

Brandon saw that the inner cave was indeed mostly water. A narrow shore of shelving rock ran all round it, but the centre was a black expanse of turgid water, glinting dangerously in the fitful light of the waving torches.

In a matter of seconds the four of them were lashed securely to stout posts of timber set upright in the rock at the edge of the underground lake. Looking round desperately, Brandon saw that Traski had now joined the sea of faces that lined the cave walls in a complete circle.

'Come to watch us die!' he grunted bleakly.

'But what will kill us?' whispered Betts. They were tied to posts about four or five yards apart.

Brandon did not answer for an instant. His eyes were riveted on the surface of the lake, striving to confirm an awful doubt that sprang from movement in the shimmering water.

Then Coralie gave a gasping cry that sounded like the echo of a whisper in the cavernous, torch-lit gloom of the dreadful place in which they stood.

'The water!' she muttered brokenly. 'Rex, it's alive with crocodiles!'

Brandon's jaw hardened. He, too, had caught a glimpse of razor-sharp teeth in a gaping mouth. As he watched in a kind of fascinated horror, he realised that Coralie was right — the water was one seething mass of giant crocs.

140

11

The Coming of Do-ana

There was something horribly impressive about the scene and the setting for the ghastly death which would presently come to Brandon and his friends. The cave, high-roofed and lit by the flaring torches round the walls, was full of faint rustling sounds. In the background the prisoners could hear the far greater noise of the constant moan from the valley. They did not know what it was; yet in itself, it made frightening music in their ears.

Brandon could not tear his eyes away from the disturbed water of the subterranean lake. It was water that held the threat of death. He knew it and shuddered at the grim notion, but refused to let despair rob him of reason. There was still a chance, he told himself. The bonds on his arms were not as tight as they should have been. He had succeeded in tautening his muscles

141

while the ropes were being tied. Now there was a certain amount of play at his wrists where they were tied to the stake.

Working with feverish energy, he struggled to loosen the cords still more.

Traski and his subjects looked on, waiting with patience for the crocodiles to make a move and carry out the sentence of death. In the meantime there arose a dirge-like chanting from the natives. The utter cheerlessness of the uncanny sound only brought greater dismay to the captives. Coralie was staring before her with wide, frightened eyes, not daring to look anywhere but at the lake. Arthur Betts blinked in the poor light. His glasses had been knocked askew so that he could not see properly. But he did not need eyesight to feel the sense of doom that was all around them.

Brandon, concentrating on trying to free one of his arms, spared little thought for anything else. He realised that time was running short. Already the giant scaly crocodiles were growing interested in the four tied prisoners. One, bolder than its fellows, came cautiously to the edge of the water, slowly and ponderously lifting its great body up on short, bowed legs.

Brandon saw the rows of teeth in its jaws, the wicked gleam of small, beady eyes.

The jaws were less than a yard from Brandon's legs.

Coralie let out a moan of pure fear. Brandon could hardly blame her, for he thought there could be nothing worse than to wait for this kind of death, watching it come closer, living through a hell of excruciating mental agony.

The cadence of the chanting rose and intensified. Several more of the crocs began to leave the water, creeping across the narrow, rocky beach towards the helpless prisoners.

Brandon cursed beneath his breath as he caught sight of a monster advancing slowly on Coralie. The girl shut her eyes, biting her lower lip to keep back the cry that rose in her throat.

Brandon fought wildly to free his arm, but still the bonds held. The crocodile closest to him took another step, its wet body glistening in the fitful light of the flares.

And all the time, the tuneless dirge of the tribesmen rose and fell around them.

'Looks like being goodbye,' called Betts.

There was a note of unconquerable courage in his voice.

'We're not dead yet!' said Brandon through his teeth. 'It's bad, but —'

His words were suddenly interrupted by a loud yell from somewhere back in the main cave. At the same time, uproar broke out among the tribe. A spotted fury with blood streaks on its side hurled itself in through the entrance of the inner cave.

'Do-ana! Do-ana!' came the cry.

'Leopard!' shouted Brandon.

'The crocs have gone back!' said Coralie.

It was true. Frightened by the sudden diversion, the scaly monsters turned tail and slithered back into the turgid water of the lake, splashing and floundering as they joined their fellow creatures again.

But it seemed as if the prisoners had merely changed one evil for another.

Bedlam reigned in the cavern. Do-ana, the leopard, was mad with pain from the wounds inflicted by the guards in the main cave. They had tried to kill the animal, but succeeded only in making it far more dangerous. Now it was causing absolute chaos, tearing round the shore of the lake and savaging several of the cornered tribesmen.

Georg Traski emptied the magazine of his automatic at the sleek, spotted shape of Do-ana, but the light was bad for accurate shooting. Only one of the bullets struck the animal. The wound was not a serious one, but served as a spur to the already mad leopard. Flicked by pain, it shot round and hurled itself at the nearest man, tearing at flesh with long raking blows of its clawed forefeet.

Tribesmen were running out through the entrance of the cave, calling to their comrades to follow, while Do-ana wrought havoc.

It was during this panic that Brandon at last succeeded in getting one of his hands free. With feverish haste he tried to untie the cords that fastened his other arm to the stake.

From the corner of his eye he saw Coralie watching him. Everything depended on his success.

But Brandon did not find his task a simple one. At any moment he knew that either the crocodiles might recover their courage, or Do-ana might launch an attack on the prisoners who, until now, had escaped the fury of its claws.

It was just then that he had a stroke of real luck in his struggle for freedom.

Terrified by the leopard, one of the natives ran blindly past Brandon, darting and dodging in an effort to keep as many obstacles as he could between himself and Do-ana.

Brandon stretched out his free hand as the man fled by. There was a jerk and the white man found himself grasping the hunting knife he had aimed for when he lunged at the man, who himself fled on, unaware of the fact that one of the prisoners was now armed.

Brandon wasted no time in slashing the rest of his bonds, before turning to his companions to sever their cords. He went to Coralie, but hardly had he started the job when the girl gave a sharp cry of warning.

'Look out behind!' yelped Betts.

Brandon whirled. His hardened body was tensed in every muscle as he found himself face to face with the pain-maddened leopard. It sprang towards him as Betts' warning rang out. Brandon ducked and side-stepped, slicing upwards with the keen blade of the hunting knife as the creature flashed past him. Then it twirled around, its feet barely touching the ground, so swift was its recovery. For an instant, Brandon felt the hot fetid breath of the animal fanning his cheek, then the knife was buried to the hilt in its side.

Thrashing wildly, the leopard tore itself clear, almost wrenching the knife from Brandon's grasp. Long curving claws ripped the flesh of his forearm. Do-ana snarled its defiance, then whipped round again and sprang to the attack once more.

Forced backwards by the rush of Do-ana, Brandon lost his footing and rolled over two or three times with the savage leopard on top of him. The animal, its coat covered in blood from wounds in its side, sought to bury its teeth in his throat. But Brandon was no mean hand at close-quarter fighting. True, he had never been involved in a mortal combat with a wounded leopard before, but many of the rules were the same.

Twisting and turning madly, man and animal pitted their skill against each other.

There could only be one end to this fight, for neither would show mercy.

He was torn and bleeding from a dozen deep scratches; but nothing could crush his determination to win.

The savage fangs snapped an inch from his face, but with superhuman strength, the man kept Do-ana at bay. Again and again he wielded the long-bladed knife, driving it hard between the leopard's ribs. But the animal, though weakening, still had plenty of power. Brandon felt the raking pain of desperate claws as they sought to rip his chest open. He winced, then held his breath as he prepared for what he hoped would be the final plunge of the knife. If only he could find the animal's heart, he thought grimly. He could not carry on much longer, for his own strength was rapidly waning.

They rolled over and over as the leopard thrashed and twisted. It gave a convulsive heave, dragging Brandon almost to the edge of the lake in its dying throes. The man tore himself free. As he did so, Do-ana's back curled and the tortured creature uttered a last long snarl of pain, then pitched over on its side with the water of the lake lapping against it.

An instant later the lake was alive with crocodiles. In less than ten seconds the body of the leopard had been dragged into the water, to be torn and fought over by the saurian monsters of the pool.

In the meantime, Brandon staggered to his feet, bleeding, battered and exhausted — but alive.

Swaying, he started forward to the wooden post where Coralie was tied. He had managed to retain the hunting knife after killing the leopard. Now he carried it in his hand and made a brave effort to grin as he reached the girl and started to cut her free. Arthur Betts was talking fast, congratulating Brandon, and N'gambi added his praise. But Brandon knew that they were by no means out of trouble.

Within seconds, the gravity of their plight was borne in on him forcibly. He felt himself seized from behind by powerful arms. Before he could show any fight, he was dragged away from Coralie and taken from the edge of the lake to the place where Georg Traski stood watching.

Brandon stared at the madman bleakly.

He was suddenly utterly weary, caring little what happened to him. After the events of the past few minutes, all the strength and vitality was sapped from his frame. A sort of numb despair swept over him. The things he had achieved were wasted, for in spite of killing Do-ana he would almost certainly be retied to the stake, alongside Coralie and the others, ready for the crocodiles to eat at their leisure.

It was a cheerless prospect and the features of Georg Traski did nothing to improve it.

Traski said: 'You are to be admired for what you have done. You and your friends have broken the laws of this realm, but honesty commands me to admire you.'

Brandon smiled thinly. A trickle of blood was running down over his eyes.

'Thanks,' he said. 'Admiration is always welcome. But in this case, I take it, it merely comes as an overture to death.' He threw his head back boldly. 'Unless your admiration can turn to an act of gratitude. Free my friends, Traski!'

Georg Traski smiled, but said nothing for a moment.

12

Sport for a King

Brandon did not expect or look for mercy for himself, but he thrust aside the weariness that oppressed him in the hope of saving his companions. Now he was fixing Traski with a coldly defiant stare, oblivious to the silence that had suddenly come down on the gathering in the cave. The only sound was the sullen splash of the crocodiles plunging about in the lake as they fought for the remnants of Do-ana.

And Georg Traski smiled.

Brandon knew his overstrung nerves were almost at breaking point. Instinctively he clenched his fists in an effort to steady himself.

Then Traski raised one hand in a queer kind of gesture.

Brandon caught his breath as the tribesmen released their hold on his arms.

He waited, not daring to move a muscle

for fear of a trick.

Traski's harsh voice echoed around the cave.

'I have said you are a brave man,' he remarked. 'I have also said that you have my admiration. Now I will go further than words. Despite the crimes you and your companions have committed against the security of my domain, I am prepared to give you all a chance to live. It will, I warn you, be a chance which will only be of use if your courage and ability are equal to the task!'

Brandon could hardly believe his ears. He squared his aching shoulders and met the madman's fanatical gaze.

'We are ready to accept the chance you offer us,' he said. 'Anything would be preferable to the barbarous sentence of death you previously issued, or the means by which it was to be carried out.'

Traski nodded. 'It is only because of your bravery and prowess that I am moved to change that decision,' he replied coldly.

'What do you propose?' asked Brandon. He had to force his voice to sound steady. His head was beginning to swim with the after-effects of his battle with the leopard, but he was no longer a prey to despair. Failure was unthinkable now. It only remained to hear the details of Traski's plan.

But Traski was in no hurry. Suddenly genial in a ghoulish fashion, he clapped his hands, ordering the attendants around him to release the other prisoners from the posts to which they were tied. Brandon could not understand the language he used, but the results made the meaning plain enough. Within a few seconds, Coralie, Arthur Betts, and N'gambi were gathered round Brandon, each one talking rapidly and asking questions he could not answer.

'You're badly hurt,' said the girl. 'Whatever happens to us afterwards they must let us dress your wounds. If they don't, you'll lose so much blood that you'll never walk out of this frightful place!'

He grinned weakly. 'Take it easy,' he advised, keeping his voice low. 'If he's as crazy as I think he is, anything could happen.'

'Do not think you are entirely free,' Traski told them in uncompromising tones. 'The great test is yet to come, but because it will be an arduous one it would be well for your friends to look after you. We will leave this cavern and return to the main cave, where food is being prepared. You may have your wounds attended to there. My people are skilled in the arts of medicine. Follow me, please.'

Eyeing each other in mute amazement, the four captives started forward in the wake of Traski as he turned and left the cave of crocodiles. Behind them came groups of tribesmen, spears at the ready. Both Brandon and Betts were wondering how strong Traski's control of his subjects might be. If their expressions were anything to go by, that control was pretty thin.

Traski motioned his prisoner-guests to couches placed against the wall on either side of his hide-covered throne. There, several women of the native tribe attended to Brandon's wounds. Although painful, none of the scratches inflicted by Do-ana proved to be more than superficial, for which he was glad. By the time the silent, unsmiling women had finished — watched closely by Coralie and the others — Brandon admitted that he felt considerably better.

By now, the meal had been brought in on great dishes of some strange metal that none of the prisoners recognised.

Brandon caught a glimpse of Traski's sadistic smile as he was examining one of the dishes. He said nothing then, but already his mind was working along lines which would later develop into something tangible — provided he could loosen up Traski sufficiently to talk more freely about his acquired kingdom.

The feast was far more welcome than might have been expected. Even N'gambi enjoyed it, though his eyes were never still as they roved about with the wariness of a hunted animal.

During the meal Brandon succeeded in getting Traski into quite a talkative mood. No mention was made on either side of the future of the prisoner-guests, but during the conversation they were able to learn a certain amount about the Valley of Devils.

It was Coralie Shaw who first broached the subject, drawing Traski out with subtly phrased remarks which whetted the foreigner's pride. She also managed to bring in the fact that her father had been a great admirer of Traski, and had perished in trying to find him.

Traski nodded slowly. 'I knew your father well,' he admitted. 'It is a pity that he should die as he did, but even if he had reached this valley I should still have been compelled to eliminate him and his party. Under no circumstances could I permit outside interference in this place.'

Brandon stepped in at that point, feeling that the talk was veering round to a dangerous subject. He was anxious to keep Traski's mind off the idea of slaughtering visitors to the valley.

'Traski,' he interjected quietly, 'there are several aspects here that intrigue us. What, for instance, causes this constant moaning noise? It began shortly after we entered the rift, and it hasn't stopped ever since. Is it some artificial device you've perfected? Or is it natural?'

Traski smirked in a superior fashion. 'You are ignorant people,' he said. 'But you couldn't know, of course. The moaning sound, which is associated with devils by the original inhabitants of this strange little valley, is caused by the night wind, which regularly comes down across the hills and plays on chimneys and rifts in the rock formation above these caves. I guessed that myself at once when I first arrived.'

Brandon smiled blandly. 'Did you have much trouble with the tribesmen of the valley?' he inquired. 'As an explorer myself, I am very interested in the adventures of others.'

Traski eyed him keenly for a moment. 'My safari was wiped out,' he said bleakly. 'You yourselves may have seen a few of the skeletons.'

'You were a lucky man to escape,' put in Coralie.

Traski spread his hands in a gesture. 'It was partly good fortune, yes,' he admitted. 'But do not think it was all down to blind luck. I am master of my own fortune! It was my own resourcefulness that saved and elevated me. I was captured after the rest of the expedition had been caught and killed. The son of the Chief was badly wounded, but I was able to make them understand that if they let me live I would heal him.'

'And you succeeded, I take it?' Brandon smiled.

Traski nodded in a self-satisfied manner. 'Naturally!' he answered. 'I used white man medicine to heal the infection that had set in. I began to learn the tribe's language. In order to ensure my own safety, I convinced the Chief that I held his son's life in my hands. He was grateful. I used this to my advantage, and when the Chief met with an ... unfortunate illness, I myself became their chief; gaining complete command over the tribe.'

Brandon considered him curiously, suspecting strongly that Traski had had a hand in this unfortunate illness that had presumably carried off the Chief.

'Why didn't you try to escape from the valley, Traski? That is something I cannot understand. You must have had many chances to walk out and return to civilisation.'

Traski grinned, his dark eyes gleaming brightly with a new, greedy light.

'Would you walk away and leave a mountain of irikum?' he demanded. 'No, my friend! Nothing but death will take me from the treasure I discovered. It is mine, and no man shall share it with me.'

Brandon understood now where the seat of Traski's madness lay; the man had a mental fixation with his precious irikum.

'You found it on your first expedition, didn't you?' he asked carefully.

Traski nodded quickly. 'In large quantities,' he said. 'We penetrated the valley and escaped with samples. It was on my second visit that disaster overcame the safari; but it was a disaster that gave me the richest treasure in the world.'

'Here in these hills?' murmured Betts, speaking for the first time.

'Here and here and here!' answered Traski loudly, throwing his arms out wide. 'This cave is hollowed from a mountain of irikum! Nowhere else in the world are there such enormous deposits!'

Brandon tried not to show his interest too openly. The greed that had sent Traski insane was also their own greatest danger, for at the slightest hint of rivalry the geologist would have them killed out of hand.

'I congratulate you, Traski,' he murmured. 'There must be few men who have met with such success. Now I can appreciate why you prefer to remain here.'

Traski nodded gravely. 'Here, I am supreme,' he said. 'No one can defy me! Nor can anyone try to usurp my power or steal my treasure. Even you and your friends will stand little chance of speaking of what you have seen in this valley. Normally you would have suffered death before now, but because of your bravery — which I admire — I am giving you a chance.'

The meal was almost at an end by this time. Brandon realised that the madman intended to reveal his plans for their future at any moment. Tension crept over him at the thought.

Traski went on with barely a pause. 'Speaking of the chance I mentioned,' he said, 'you are probably interested in what I propose.'

Brandon said nothing, but nodded wordlessly.

Arthur Betts blinked in the torch-lit cave.

Coralie bit her lower lip in silence.

N'gambi waited, tense but silent.

Traski said: 'You will all be allowed an hour's rest. Then my men will wake you. You will be permitted to take one rifle each, with two rounds of ammunition for each weapon. Then you will walk out of here, free people.' The flicker of a cunning smile touched his bearded face as he finished.

Brandon cleared his throat noisily. 'Free?' he murmured somewhat doubtfully. 'What do you mean by that exactly?'

Traski shrugged his broad shoulders. 'You will be free to make your way from the Valley of Devils,' he replied. Then added: 'If you are swift enough on your feet, that is.'

'I see.' Brandon's voice was hard. 'And how fast shall we have to move?'

'How can I tell? When you leave this cave no effort will be made to stop you. But ...' He paused significantly. 'At the end of thirty minutes from the time of your going, my hunters will be out. If you can reach the mouth of the valley in half an hour, all well and good. If not, you and your friends will be fair game for the chase. Clear?'

Brandon gritted his teeth. 'Perfectly, thank you,' he answered. 'You yourself will naturally join the hunt, I take it?'

Traski smiled. 'But of course! Is not hunting a sport fit for kings, my friend?'

13

Big Game!

There was a spell of silence that continued for a long time when Georg Traski finished speaking.

Brandon glanced sideways at Coralie. Betts looked at N'gambi with a frown. At length it was Brandon who opened his mouth as the atmosphere of suspense increased.

'So you intend to use us as big game,' he murmured quietly.

Traski made a deprecating motion with his left hand.

'Perhaps you could call it that,' he admitted slowly. 'But you will not be unarmed, remember. Between you, you will have four rifles and eight rounds of ammunition. It would be poor sport indeed to hunt creatures without giving them a chance to defend themselves — or even escape.'

Brandon sniffed audibly. 'Half an hour

won't be long in which to leave this valley,' he observed. 'It's a full hour's march to the entrance from here, and you know it! Aren't you making mighty sure that we don't get away?'

Traski smiled disarmingly. 'I warned you,' he said simply. 'If you do not relish the idea there is no reason why I should not return you immediately to the lake of the crocodiles. I am offering you a sporting chance; you need not accept it!'

'We'll accept it all right!' retorted Brandon grimly. 'We might even win; you never know!'

Traski inclined his head gravely. 'That is well,' he replied. 'I wish you success — and the luck you need.'

'Thanks,' said Arthur Betts. 'It will certainly be a new experience to be the hunted rather than the hunter!'

'My hunters are good,' answered Traski quietly. 'Do not underrate their ability, my friends.'

Betts smiled. 'They didn't show up so well when Do-ana appeared on the scene,' he pointed out, cuttingly

Traski ignored the thrust. But in spite

of Betts' brave words the prisoners knew well enough that they would be up against heavy odds when the time came. Half an hour would not be nearly long enough to escape from the steep-sided Valley of Devils; when the tribesmen hunted them down the eight rounds of ammunition they were to be allowed would make little difference.

However, none of them permitted themselves to lose heart. At least they would be free for a short while, and all the time freedom was theirs, defeat and death might be changed to escape and success.

Brandon rose stiffly to his feet. The wounds he had suffered at the claws of Doana were not nearly so painful as he would have expected. It said a great deal for the medicine of the tribesmen, and Brandon was duly grateful.

'We accept your terms, Traski,' he said. 'In view of the lateness of the hour and our fatigue, may I suggest that we be allowed to take our rest?'

Traski nodded permission, then held up his hand for silence. He, too, rose from his throne and stood facing his captive-guests, a full drinking gourd in one hand.

'First let us drink to the thrill of the chase,' he said.

Brandon glanced at the girl, who shuddered slightly. But she raised her drink in silence none the less. It was a strange toast — the hunter drinking to the hunted. Brandon would have remarked on it had the circumstances been somewhat different. As it was, he felt tiredness creeping over him again. The strain of his recent experiences was telling on him. He knew that unless he got some sleep, he would not be a fit leader for the little party when they left the cave and sought to save their lives.

Traski raised no objection. In fact, he tried to put them at their ease as quickly as he could. Summoning some of his henchmen, he gave orders for the prisoners to be given couches on which to sleep. Then he stood in front of Brandon and bowed his head a little.

'Make good use of your respite,' he advised. 'You will leave this cave in darkness, but dawn will be breaking by the time your thirty minutes' grace has elapsed. I myself shall come to see you off and bid you *bon chance*. Now rest in peace while

166

you have the chance.'

Betts and Brandon acknowledged the madman's words with sceptical smiles. Coralie thanked him quietly, while N'gambi ducked his head in sober silence.

Then Traski turned and left them, making his way outside the cave into the darkness of the night.

Brandon walked slowly towards the entrance. He found Coralie at his elbow. Behind them, piles of skins were being brought in for use as beds.

'So, now we know what we're up against,' murmured the girl. She did not sound unduly disturbed. Perhaps she was putting more faith in Brandon's ability as a leader than she should have done. Brandon did not know, but he played up to her optimism for all that.

'How do you feel?' he asked gently. 'This is a bit on the sticky side, isn't it?' He grinned as he said it.

'We'll get through,' she said firmly. 'I can feel it in my bones, Rex!'

They were almost at the mouth of the cave. Brandon guessed that the entrance would be guarded. He was not intending to make a break for it in any event, but as if to deter him, the shadowy figure of a tall tribesman drifted into view from the boulders and scrub at one side of the cave mouth. He was joined by a second man who came to meet him. They paused and stood together for a moment, speaking quietly and glancing into the cave every now and again.

Brandon jerked his head towards them. 'Taking no chances,' he breathed. 'This Traski fellow is certainly a queer bird, I must say.'

'He's crazy, of course,' she answered. 'The irikum, I suppose. A sort of fanatical desire to keep what he's found and not let anyone else get their hands on it.'

'That's it, all right!' agreed Brandon grimly. 'He doesn't intend us to get away if he can help it!'

Coralie frowned. 'Do you think he'll stick to his side of the bargain?' she asked. 'I mean, is he likely to pull off a trick and have us killed before we get a hundred yards?'

The same thought had occurred to Brandon, though he didn't admit this to Coralie. Instead, he said, 'I think he's a man who will stick to the rules.'

She nodded. 'I hope you're right, Rex.' Her arm was linked through his. 'Let's go back and get some sleep.'

They turned, withdrawing into the cool of the cave, and joined Betts and N'gambi, who were already settling down on their beds of skins. Brief goodnights were said; no one seemed inclined to discuss the immediate future.

Brandon, lying on his back and staring up at the high roof of the cavern, found sleep hard to woo. His mind repeatedly turned to the coming ordeal, seeking to think of some way in which he would be able to turn the tables on Traski. Then sleep overtook him of its own accord.

The next thing he knew, was being shaken into wakefulness by a tall tribesman, who grinned down at his face when he opened his eyes.

'So soon!' he muttered ruefully. Glancing round he saw that his companions had already been roused. Near the mouth of the cave stood Traski, while behind him were four of his men, each bearing a rifle.

'You were undisturbed?' Traski asked. He

sounded as if he was in excellent humour. Brandon glared at him.

'We slept,' Brandon answered tartly. 'Now we're ready to leave.'

Traski nodded sagely. The four people received their rifles and ammunition.

'We trust you,' said Brandon. 'No attempt will be made to recapture us for thirty minutes, is it understood?'

'Agreed,' said Traski gravely. 'I am a man of my word, do not fear. But when the time is up you will be hunted with utter ruthlessness. Should you escape by any chance, my reign as King of the Valley of Devils will be over. I do not think you will escape; but by all means try.'

'We will!' grunted Brandon. He glanced at the others. 'All right?' he inquired. They nodded wordlessly. With a final glance at Traski, Brandon led his party out into the dark of night beyond the cave mouth. Standing in full war array, the tribesmen and hunters of the Valley of Devils were drawn up in a great semi-circle to watch their departure.

'Run as fast as you can!' Brandon ordered. He himself led the way, making in the direction of the valley entrance.

When he had covered a hundred yards of the tangled jungle pathway he slowed down and halted.

'What's the idea?' panted Betts. 'If we ran all the way, we shouldn't get out in half an hour! That was a waste of breath!'

Brandon grinned in the gloom. 'I don't think so,' he answered. 'Maybe Traski will think that's exactly what we mean to do — run all the way. I've got a better idea, if the rest of you agree.'

'Anything you say, Rex,' said Coralie quietly.

Brandon set off again down the path, walking this time. The sky was already lightening a little as they glimpsed it through the overhanging trees. But Brandon gave only a passing thought to time.

'I seem to remember seeing something about a mile before we arrived at the cave,' he said quietly. 'There's no possible chance of getting out of the valley in half an hour of course, but we may be able to fox the hunters another way.'

Beyond that he would say no more about his plan. They hurried on as silently as they could. Ten precious minutes had slipped by already.

Presently Brandon stopped again, motioning N'gambi to join him. Lying beside the narrow path, partly covered in undergrowth, was a fallen tree trunk.

'Can we rig up a dead-fall?' asked Brandon.

N'gambi nodded understandingly. 'Sure,' he answered quickly.

Betts caught on just as rapidly. While Coralie stood guard with one of the rifles, the three men heaved and struggled with the dead tree until they had manoeuvred it across the path and fixed it with a slender trigger of wood. A strand of liana was attached to the trigger and stretched across the pathway. Provided the trip was operated before dawn revealed the dead-fall, it would be a useful weapon.

'Now for the actual escape plan' said Brandon, satisfied with what he had done so far. It was not a lot, but he felt it was worth the time sacrificed to carry it out.

The rest of them looked at him inquiringly. Coralie's eyes were bright with eagerness. Her faith in Brandon was complete. He hoped he wouldn't let her down too badly.

'Come on,' he said grimly. 'There's just about one place in this valley where we can scale the side and get out if we're lucky. I happened to notice it when they brought us along here. Now we've got to make a break for it!'

Betts gave a chuckle of approval. 'So Traski will be hunting us through the valley while we're streaking away at right angles.'

They were already moving again, following Brandon as he led the way down the path.

'Don't be too sure of anything,' he warned them. 'We still have to climb the side for one thing, and the hunt's due to begin in less than fifteen minutes. They'll track us, naturally, and we can't hope to throw them off for long. It's just a matter of moving fast and getting clear before they catch up with us. Once we're out of this death-trap valley, things won't be nearly so bad.'

Straining his eyes in the gradually lightening gloom, Brandon finally located the place he had had in mind. It was one of the few spots in the valley walls where undergrowth did not grow quite so thickly. In the darkness of the previous night he had glimpsed a certain bareness about it, and now it proved to be what he had prayed for — a fault in the side of the steep wall up which it would be possible for determined people to scramble.

When they reached it and started the climb he checked his watch, seeing by the luminous hands that it wanted no more than seven and a half minutes before their half hour's grace was up.

Gritting his teeth, he led the way up the lower slope. The sky was showing the first hints of light. They felt time slipping past and over them as they sweated and toiled up the steep, rugged escarpment of the valley side.

Less than a quarter of the way to the top, and freedom, they heard the long-drawn note of a horn, followed immediately by faint but clearly audible shouting from the direction of the bowl-shaped end of the defile.

Brandon stole a quick look at his watch.

'They've started!' he grunted breathlessly. 'Dead on time, too!'

'Keep going,' panted Coralie, right behind him.

N'gambi, throwing glances over his shoulder, followed the girl, with Arthur Betts bringing up the rear. Encumbered by their rifles, they struggled upwards. With freedom almost in sight at the top of the climb it seemed incredible that the men in the valley below should outwit them now, but Brandon realised that a lot could happen before they reached their goal. From below they were exposed to arrows if the tribal hunters spotted them, yet they could not waste too much time on caution. Speed alone would save them.

'We've nearly done it!' gasped Coralie. 'Just a few more feet to go, Rex!'

Brandon said nothing, conserving his strength for the final sharp climb. Then he was heaving his body over the edge of the valley wall, to lie panting on the ground as the others joined him, exhausted. For several seconds none of them caught sight of Georg Traski.

When they did, he had them covered with his ready automatic.

14

The Law of the Knife

A red haze of anger swirled in Brandon's mind as he focused on the madman. He swore beneath his breath, but bodily exhaustion pressed him down on the ground with a weight that was almost physical.

Time stood still. It was just as if Brandon and his friends were suddenly suspended in a vacuum.

Then Coralie sobbed in a broken, unintelligible whisper.

The sound brought Brandon reeling back to full awareness. He straggled up to his knees and sought to bring his rifle up to fire from the hip before Traski got him. But the move was too late. From scrub and thorn on either side of the spot where Traski was standing, his tribesmen appeared, screening their ruler before Brandon could pull the trigger.

'Wait!' said Betts. 'They'll kill us out of

hand if you fire!'

'Maybe better that way,' grunted Brandon. He knew he had failed, and failure was a bitter thing. Traski had obviously anticipated the plan he had formed. With a sick sense of despair, he lowered his rifle and waited. Behind them was the almost sheer drop to the valley floor; in front stood the tribesmen, watchful and alert, their spears and bows and arrows stiffly aimed.

'The choice of two evils,' muttered Betts grimly. 'To die where we are or be killed later on. Which?'

'I can't make a choice,' said Brandon. 'That sort of thing is a personal matter.'

Very slowly, still grasping his rifle, he got to his feet.

'Traski!' he shouted. 'Come out from behind these men of yours! You've got us cornered; but we aren't dead yet and we've still got eight rounds left!'

'But you will die!' came Traski's answer.

'Don't be too sure!' retorted Betts before Brandon could reply.

'The moment any of you fire a gun, you will all die,' said Traski curtly. 'It is stalemate, I think, but the odds are heavily in my favour. Again, you are brave and win my admiration.'

'Show yourself!' said Brandon 'I never took you for a coward, Traski, villain though you are.'

The taunt had the desired effect this time. Brandon had hardly expected it, but Georg Traski thrust his way between the ranks of his men and confronted the cornered group at the edge of the valley wall. He carried automatics in both hands, and clearly would not hesitate to use them at the slightest provocation. Brandon kept his finger curled about the trigger of his rifle, but he noticed that Traski was pointing one of his pistols directly at Coralie. To make any move himself would bring instant death to the girl. It was a chance he could not take.

'Well?' he demanded. 'What are your terms?'

Traski raised his eyebrows slightly. 'Terms?' he echoed. 'I cannot remember offering any.'

'But you will! There'd be no satisfaction in killing us off after such an easy victory, would there? You're not a man who welcomes easy victories, Traski. You're a king, and kings defend their titles in such a way as to impress their subjects.'

Traski frowned. 'I am their master!' he snapped.

'But you couldn't kill the leopard in the cave,' sneered Brandon. 'Even with your automatic you failed. Don't you think they've lost a little of their faith in you?'

'They respect me as their king!' retorted Traski thinly.

Brandon realised he would have to be careful. Pushed much further, the madman would fire. Brandon didn't want that to happen. He was hoping for still another chance. It was suddenly tremendously important to go on living.

'These people respect courage,' he said softly. 'I do not think you have sufficient to retain their respect without proving me wrong.'

'You lie!' whispered Traski. 'I have more courage in me than you ever had!'

'Why not prove it to your subjects then?'

Traski stiffened. For an instant his knuckles showed tense and white as he squeezed on the triggers of his guns. But he didn't fire. Instead he suddenly threw back his head and laughed in a wild, insane fashion.

'And why not?' he demanded loudly. 'By killing you in single combat I shall restore to my people their faith in my reign!'

Brandon drew a long breath that was part relief and part excitement.

'And the terms of this duel?' he queried. 'What are they?'

'The choice shall be yours,' replied Traski with a smile. It was plain that he already felt confidence lift him up on the wings of victory.

Brandon hesitated for just an instant.

'Knives,' he said quietly. 'We fight with knives, King Traski!'

Traski caught his breath, but there was no backing down. Some of his men had gathered the gist by now. At the word 'knives' they grinned in anticipation.

'As you wish,' said Traski. A glance had shown him the reactions of his people. 'We shall fight with knives.'

Brandon shot a reassuring look at Coralie and Betts, who had both turned pale when he made his choice of weapon.

'That is settled,' he said grimly. 'And the victor's reward?'

Traski sneered. 'I am already the victor!' he snapped. 'My reward will be the increased love of my tribesmen.'

Brandon smiled slightly. 'But suppose for argument's sake that you lost ... Will you make it plain to your men that *I* will then take your place?'

Traski hesitated for a moment, then turned towards the men gathered behind him. He spoke for several seconds, gesturing to Brandon and the valley below. Was he imparting Brandon's terms?

Coralie was pleading with Brandon to be careful. Betts was whispering advice that Brandon barely heard. Only N'gambi caught his attention.

'You will win, *bwana*,' he said. 'If you do not we shall sell our lives for as many of these pigs as we have bullets!'

'Thanks,' muttered Brandon. 'I'll do my best.'

'Are you ready?' asked Traski with an evil grin. 'Tell your friends to drop their rifles.'

'No,' answered Brandon firmly. 'It is only you and I who will dispense with firearms.'

Traski shrugged. Watching Brandon, he lowered his two automatics very slowly.

Brandon let his rifle sag. The weapons touched the ground at the same instant. Then Traski and Brandon stepped towards each other, away from the guns.

Traski clapped his hands and one of the tribesmen ran forward with a pair of long-bladed hunting knives. He offered one to his master, the other to Brandon.

Brandon took the weapon, balanced it in his strong brown hand and examined the blade with narrowed eyes. There was nothing wrong with it. Then he looked up and saw that the men had closed in, forming a semi-circle from the edge of the valley wall drop. Coralie, Betts and N'gambi were in the cut off sector, as were Traski and himself. The stage was set. A half-circle of spear blades confined the protagonists, ensuring that neither retreated too far.

Very slowly, Traski started to move around Brandon. The madman had put off his robe and now appeared in stained breeches and tattered bush shirt. His eyes were aflame and his teeth showed white through the ragged growth of his beard.

Brandon realised that Traski was immensely strong, while he himself had been seriously weakened by loss of blood and the strain of his recent exertions.

Brandon tested his adversary's speed a couple of times by making sudden lunges before leaping back. Traski was swift, but not more so than Brandon. Brandon whirled in and drove him back almost to the ring of spear blades. Traski dropped onto one knee and thrust upwards as Brandon closed.

The keen steel of his knife passed through Brandon's shirt and touched the skin of his side with an icy finger. Brandon hurled himself away as Traski twisted the knife in an effort to bury it in his body. At the same time, his free hand gripped Traski's wrist and held it. Their knife hands were locked together as Brandon slowly but surely forced Traski's knife away from him. Then Traski brought his leg up and round, catching Brandon behind the knees and jerking him forward. Brandon overbalanced and fell. He rolled aside wildly as Traski threw himself on top of him. They were fighting in a clinch as they rolled this way and that, first one, then the other on top. But neither man gave sufficient time for the other to bring his knife into play.

Then Brandon drew blood for the first time. He leapt to his feet after throwing Traski off. Before Traski could recover, Brandon dived full on to him, gleaming blade thrust out as he dropped. Traski uttered a stifled cry as the steel bit his flesh and bared his shoulder. But Brandon's aim had been imperfect. Traski was only maddened by the pain of the wound.

He sprang up before Brandon could strike again, and an instant later the two of them were fighting close together once more. Brandon felt his knife hand being forced backwards by the powerful muscles of Traski's free hand. But he was doing the same to Traski. Traski suddenly and unexpectedly relaxed his knife arm, so that Brandon almost fell against him. At the last moment he managed to keep his balance, while Traski was forced half round by his own manoeuvre, so losing the advantage of the trick.

Brandon followed it up by a swift thrust at Traski's ribs. The blow connected, but was not deep enough to do much harm. Traski gasped and bit his lip, then began swearing at Brandon in his own language. Brandon forced him further and further backwards.

Traski threw a hurried glance over his shoulder, seeing the edge of the drop a few feet away. He made a wild and desperate slicing movement with his knife. Brandon saw it coming, ducked his head and parried the blow with his own weapon. Traski screamed. His knife dropped to the ground from nerveless fingers as he stared aghast at the spurt of arterial blood that gushed from his wrist.

A great shout went up all round them. Only Traski did not seem to notice it. He was beginning to sway as his life's blood spurted out in scarlet gouts. With a weak effort, he clapped his other hand over the wound, but still the blood was pumped out. Tottering now, he staggered backwards, eyes glazing over.

Brandon stood rigidly, watching him with a fascinated stare. Then Traski collapsed as he reached the edge of the drop at his back. With a rapidly fading cry he made a vain attempt to save himself from falling. No one tried to help him. He was probably already dead when he landed in the scrub-choked valley below.

Brandon, his senses swimming, sank slowly to his knees as Coralie ran forward and threw her arms round his neck. Her eyes were wet with tears of relief. Betts was wringing his hand; N'gambi was doing a sort of dance in front of him.

The tribesmen were chanting a song of victory as they advanced still more tightly round the four elated people. Traski's blood was spattered thickly on the ground.

Brandon put Coralie gently away. He stood up and faced the men, squaring his aching shoulders defiantly, not yet sure whether they would accept him as the victor. The chanting ceased as they met his gaze, then one of them, a massively built man with gleaming skin and large, bold eyes, took a step forward, halting before him. His spear was raised in sombre greeting, the butt towards Brandon.

Brandon heaved a sigh of relief. He stooped and picked up his knife, the blade still wet with Traski's blood. Very gravely, he held it out to the man, hilt first. The man bowed, took the knife, touched his forehead with the blade and passed it back. For the first time he grinned. Turning to his fellows, he lifted his spear up high and uttered a peculiar shout which was instantly echoed by the rest. It rang out again and again in the silence of the forest. Brandon did not have to be a linguist to translate its meaning.

'Rex Brandon, King of the Valley of Devils!' It was Coralie Shaw who spoke.

Betts whistled between his teeth and blinked in the early morning light.

'Congratulations, Rex,' he said. 'You're living up to your name, I see!'

Brandon laughed. Before they could discuss the matter more deeply, they were urged to leave the spot and return by a secret path to the caves of the valley. Here, they were feasted with great ceremony, and here they stayed as they began to recover from their recent ordeals.

By the end of a week they were conversant enough with the language of the tribe to get by. During those days of rest they explored the valley thoroughly, taking samples of the mineral deposits of irikum. Betts had the time of his life listing and classifying the fauna of the place; while Coralie shared with Brandon the excitement of geological wealth. Even N'gambi was happy.

But the time came at last when Brandon decided they must leave.

Gathering the tribe together, he addressed them. At his side stood Stromwhi, the tall man who had first acclaimed him king.

'I and my friends must leave you. I am not your rightful Chief. This man, Stromwhi, is your rightful ruler. This man, Stromwhi, is the son of your Chief who ruled at the time of Traski's arrival. This man, Stromwhi, is the real heir to the throne of the Valley of Devils!

'I will return, with others. Your land holds many riches, which white men covet. We, the white men, will pay you for the right to take away the dark rock of the caves. Will you give us safe passage?'

There was a moment's silence, then Stromwhi gave a lead to his people, accepting Brandon's terms and giving his trust.

Brandon and the others were soon

189

afterwards escorted down the valley path. When they left it, they did so with mixed feelings.

'I'm glad we found Traski,' said Coralie quietly. 'And I'm glad I came here with you, Rex. Your objectives were the same as my father's. It seems oddly just that I should share your success as I would have shared his.'

Brandon turned his head and smiled down at her. Then he took her hand in his and pressed it firmly. 'Sort of partners, aren't we?' he grinned.

'You can buy me another gramophone out of the proceeds!' put in Arthur Betts in a slightly pained voice.

N'gambi gave a loud laugh as the forest swallowed them, a forest that stretched for many miles between themselves and their final destination — home.

We do hope that you have enjoyed reading this large print book.

Did you know that all of our titles are available for purchase?

We publish a wide range of high quality large print books including:
Romances, Mysteries, Classics
General Fiction
Non Fiction and Westerns

Special interest titles available in large print are:
The Little Oxford Dictionary
Music Book, Song Book
Hymn Book, Service Book

Also available from us courtesy of Oxford University Press:
Young Readers' Dictionary
(large print edition)
Young Readers' Thesaurus
(large print edition)

For further information or a free brochure, please contact us at:
Ulverscroft Large Print Books Ltd.,
The Green, Bradgate Road, Anstey,
Leicester, LE7 7FU, England.
Tel: (00 44) **0116 236 4325**
Fax: (00 44) **0116 234 0205**

Other titles in the
Linford Mystery Library:

A FROZEN SILENCE

Arlette Lees

Deputies Frack Tilsley and Robely Danner are called to a remote section of woods outside their small farming community of Abundance, Wisconsin, where a man stands handcuffed and frozen to a tree. As they investigate this brutal murder, a young woman discovers the purse of a missing secretary from nearby Promontory which contains a cryptic diary. Digging deeper, Tilsley and Danner discover common denominators linking several suspects to two murder victims and possibly a third, with the chief of police himself on their list . . .

THE LADY OF DOOM

Gerald Verner

Whispers have reached Scotland Yard of an elusive figure that has appeared on the dark horizon of crime and is making its influence felt. Then the first threatening letter comes, demanding a huge payment, or death for its recipient. The victim goes to the police for protection — only to be promptly murdered. The same graft has been worked by gangsters in Chicago — and now it seems they have arrived in London. As Scotland Yard strives to find the criminal mastermind responsible, so too does a mysterious woman . . . the Lady of Doom!

RENDEZVOUS WITH A CORPSE

Fletcher Flora

The wayward beauty who comes back to her old hometown to titillate her ex-boyfriend (now a married lawyer) and to blackmail her ex-husband is ripe bait for murder. And murder is just what she gets. Suspicion falls heaviest on the old flame: he was at the scene of the crime and out of his legal mind, befuddled by a number of potent cocktails. The police find his explanation incredible; but his wife, believing in his innocence, sets out to pursue an investigation of her own . . .